MIDNIGHT OFFENSIVE

ELLE E. KAY

Blessings!

Elle E. Kay

Midnight Offensive

Faith Writes Publishing

PO BOX 494

BENTON PA 17814-0494

Ebook ISBN: 978-1-950240-47-0

Paperback ISBN: 978-1-950240-48-7

Acknowledgements

First, heartfelt thanks to my husband, Joe Kelleher—your steady encouragement keeps me writing when deadlines loom and coffee runs low.

A special shout-out to my fabulous editor, Patti Geesey. Your sharp eye makes every story stronger. Any lingering errors are mine alone.

To my beta team—thank you for catching the little things before anyone else sees them. And to my ARC readers and street team, your reviews and word-of-mouth support mean the world to me.

Finally, thank you, dear readers. Your enthusiasm allows me to keep doing what I love. My prayer is that these stories entertain you and, more importantly, draw hearts closer to the Lord Jesus Christ.

This book is a work of fiction. Names, characters, businesses, places, events, and incidents are either products of the author's imagination or, where real, used

Dedication

I dedicate this book to my fellow writers and friends at American Christian Fiction Writers (ACFW).

EPIGRAPH

"But now, O LORD, thou *art* our father; we *are* the clay, and thou our potter; and we all *are* the work of thy hand."

—Isaiah 64:8 (KJV)

Chapter One

"Code black. Code black." The tinny voice sounded over the loudspeaker system, interrupting Sadie's roommate Madison's rousing rendition of "Leroy the Redneck Reindeer." They were attending a holiday party in their break room.

Sadie and her coworkers shared concerned glances as they rushed to the nurses' station to receive their instructions.

"We're looking at a multi-vehicle accident. A bus was involved along with a mini-van carrying a family with young children. Let's get ready for them." The charge nurse lifted her chin, dismissing them.

Sadie's throat constricted and a knot formed in her stomach. Cases involving kids hit her the hardest.

The beeping of monitors and the shouts of doctors and nurses clamoring to prepare for the expected arrivals were at odds with the festive colored lights and the plate filled with delicious gingerbread men they'd left behind.

As she entered the fray and faced the harsh lighting of the ED, the pursed lips and furrowed brow of the general surgeon on duty made it clear she was waiting on a patient with life-threatening complications.

Details trickled in, and soon they had an idea of what happened at the scene. A car sideswiped a bus full of Bucknell students, pushing it into the wrong lane on I-80 where it collided with a mini-van carrying a family of six. Several other vehicles were involved to a lesser degree. A few would go to Evan. Evangelical Community Hospital. However, the worst cases would be transported here. Life flight was two minutes out with their youngest patient.

As usual, they were short-staffed. Her sensible shoes squeaked on the waxed floors as she hurried to the elevator and hit the button that would open its doors. She stepped in, drew in a sharp breath of stale sterile air, counted to ten, and prepared to meet the chopper. On the roof, the whir of the blades drowned out all other noise and she had to hang on to doors to remain steady while standing on the helipad. Her fingers clenched and unclenched waiting for the blades to slow.

The coppery smell of blood hit her when she moved toward her patient.

The EMT hopped from the chopper, clipboard in hand. "Head wound. Suspected liver trauma."

She gave him a curt nod, fingers traveling to the boy's wrist to get his pulse. Thready. His skin was cool to the touch. She swiveled to face the EMT. "Let's get him inside."

If not for the car seat, how much worse could it have been? His siblings walked away unharmed. The parents were a different story. She lifted a prayer for the family.

They walked on either side, carrying the seven-year-old boy and rode the elevator silently down to the ED. Once there, she checked his vitals again. BP had dropped. Far too low. The EMT administered fluids and they'd continue to do the same, but there wasn't much she could do for him. He needed to see the doctor and get prepped for surgery.

Sadie took a deep breath to steady herself and went to find the doctor, weaving through overcrowded halls. The frantic beeps of machines and the low murmur of voices followed her through the department as she searched. "Dr. Li. The seven-year-old patient who was brought in by life flight is ready for you. BP is falling fast."

Whatever happened next would depend on her and the surgical team. Sadie checked with triage to find out where she was most needed.

The non-alcoholic eggnog she'd chugged earlier soured in her stomach, so she fought to keep it down.

It was impossible to remain detached despite her best intentions. Her parents had warned her to choose a different career. They told her that soft hearts like hers needed careers in the arts, not working in a level-one trauma center. But places like this needed empathetic souls to care for their patients and pray for them when they were at their worst. If she prayed out loud, she could lose her job. Unless a patient asked for prayer. Then she could get away with it. But she needed to be wise about it. What was that verse? Something about being wise as a serpent and harmless as a dove. That was her goal in life.

Sirens sounded in the distance. The first ambulance was seconds away.

ALHAD SHARMA WOULD'VE PREFERRED to avoid the emergency department, but refusing medical attention would've brought unwanted attention from the first responders. So, he answered the intake questions, and didn't waver one bit as he gave them a false name. Adam Smith. He didn't look like an Adam Smith, but in America, it worked. And it was only one of many stolen identities he'd secured to help him get through his mission. Careful planning had gone into each and every step of his plan. Shady back-room dealings in the seediest part of Baltimore where desperation settled into the corners and chased the brave few who dared attempt escape. He'd acquired the necessary documents. Although, his brother would need to secure the identity that would get him out of the country. It was too risky to use one that might get flagged.

Soon he would relocate to a tropical paradise about as far from ground zero as possible. That way, when the winning bidder took their revenge against the United States, he would be out of harm's way.

Alexei Ivanov, Wei Zhang, and Ahmed Al-Mansour all fought for exclusive rights to his formula. Only one would prevail.

The mixed scents in the hospital competed for attention, but the strong odor of antiseptic overpowered even the floor wax and the faint touches of burned flesh, urine, and blood that hung in the air. No doubt from the victims of the crash who'd been more severely injured than he had.

Once inside a room, he changed out of his bloody clothing into the cheap cotton gown. His stomach clenched as he glanced around and realized his case was missing. Javier had walked away unscathed, so he would have it with any luck. He crawled under starchy sheets that scratched his already tender skin.

A few minutes passed before a woman in scrubs entered his room.

"When will the doctor be in?" He sat up taller in the bed, wincing, his hand flying to his ribs.

"You're looking at her."

A female doctor. Great. Just perfect. A man with a direct approach would be better. He didn't have the energy to attempt to read between the lines.

The woman performed a cursory examination and clucked her tongue against the roof of her mouth. "Your injuries are consistent with those we frequently see from seat belts and airbags. We'll get an MRI to make sure there is no internal damage, but it may be a few hours until that's possible, so you'll need to sit tight."

After jotting something on a clipboard, she trotted

away. He closed his eyes against the pain throbbing through his skull, and when he reopened them, Javier García stepped into his room, the clack of his boots disturbing the relative quiet.

"What took you so long?" He hissed the words through his teeth. "We should leave."

"It'll seem suspicious if you leave before morning. I overheard the police claiming you're responsible for the accident, so if you leave too soon, they're going to come calling."

"I can't let that metal case get into the wrong hands." He gripped the rail of his bed until his knuckles turned white.

"It's secured."

Alhad leaned forward, his eyes narrowing. "Secured where?"

Javier chuckled, but there was no humor in his laugh. "Don't you trust me, boss?" The glint in his eyes held a warning.

Alhad clenched his jaw. Their business arrangement wasn't the type that inspired faith in humanity. "I trust nobody."

"Smart." The big man moved closer, using his physical prowess to intimidate him. It was typical for a thug like him, but Alhad refused to show him any fear. He kept eye contact and attempted to mask the slight tremble of his hands by shoving them beneath the rough sheet. He had no use for bullies. Unless of course, they were doing his bidding. Javier was on his payroll, and he needed to make sure he knew who signed his paycheck. Not that he'd ever see a cent. But he didn't know he was a disposable tool.

"As long as you hold up your end of our bargain, I'll keep you and your precious metal briefcase safe," Javier said.

Twenty percent of his profit. It was an exorbitant cost for protection, but if you wanted good help, you had to make believe you were going to pay for it. A bullet between the eyes would rid him of Javier without costing him a cent if it came to that. But he had something else in mind. When the time was right, he'd make his move.

AFTER TWELVE HOURS OF overtime, Sadie checked the vitals of one final patient before calling it a night. Madison lounged against the nurses' station, waiting for her.

"What did you think of him?"

She rested against the counter beside her friend, struggling to stay upright. "Him? Him who?"

"The guy whose room you just exited."

Sadie rubbed her eyes and took a moment to remember where she'd come from before answering. "I didn't give him much thought at all, to be honest. My brain is fuzzy. The only thing I want to think about is going to sleep." Her eyelids drooped at the thought.

"Well, the guy in there gives me the creeps."

"We're not supposed to say things like that about our patients, Mads."

"I know." She stuck out her lip and crinkled her nose.

"He was driving the car, you know. The one that caused this whole mess."

"It's not our place to judge him." Sadie stretched and yawned. "The law will sort it out."

"You don't really believe that, do you? The whole 'justice will prevail' mantra."

"I don't know." She peered up at her friend. "Can we go home now?"

"Yes, please." Madison looked down on Sadie from her lofty 5'10" height. "Give me your keys. No way am I letting you drive me anywhere in your condition."

Sadie fished them from her purse and deposited them in her friend's hand. "The question is why aren't you about to fall over? We've both been here for twenty-four hours straight."

Madison flipped the keys into the air and caught them before they could fall to the ground. "I took a twenty-minute nap in one of the on-call rooms a few hours ago. Gave me my second wind."

Another yawn escaped. "That never works for me. A few minutes of shut-eye only leaves me groggier than I started."

CRAIG MALONE SCANNED THE brightly lit corridor, a habit he'd developed when he joined the military. It served him well in his job as Tactical Operations Leader for Homeland Security. His desk chair squeaked as he pushed to his feet. Inside the room behind him, a team led by Dr. Matthew Wright worked to finalize an antidote for Viper-X, a biological weapon stolen from a lab located in New Mexico's Jemez Mountains.

The government had believed that facility to be secure, too. A mistake. They hadn't counted on an inside job by Dr. Alhad Sharma, an expert in infectious diseases and genetic engineering. He'd broken their trust and absconded with the weaponized virus.

Craig's job here in Pennsylvania was to keep the researchers, especially Dr. Matthew Wright from stealing their own work product—the antidote to Viper-X. He and Matt had become friends in the short time they'd known each other, but that friendship wouldn't cause him to let down his guard. Loyalty to country was ingrained into him, not only from his time serving as a Navy SEAL, but it was passed down from his father and his grandfather before him.

Matt inched the door open and stuck his head out. "It's still you out here, huh?"

"Wishing your agent was someone prettier?"

"Lisa is far better to look at, but I don't think Madison would be thrilled about me making friends with her, so you'll have to do."

Craig chuckled. "How's the research coming along?"

"Making remarkable progress. Now that we're past the initial in vitro testing, the mice not only survived, but showed no adverse effects. Rabbits did well also."

Craig crinkled his nose. "Don't you hate testing on animals?"

"It's critical to providing safe and effective treatment

for humans, so we do so ethically, following strict guidelines in an effort to minimize any discomfort. The animals are well cared for."

"I get that, but I couldn't do what you do."

"This type of research isn't for everyone."

"What's next?"

"We'll be moving on to larger animal trials."

"How long will that process take?"

"I'd like to have several years for the tests, but given the time sensitive nature, I'll accelerate the process."

"I hope you mean by cutting it down to weeks, not months or years."

"Your bosses aren't giving me much of a choice in the matter. They think it's ready and want to make sure it'll work in humans."

"Will you do human testing?"

"We won't intentionally infect someone, but if Viper-X gets released somehow, my antidote may be their only hope of survival."

Craig sat back in his chair, gazing at the flickering light overhead. "That's quite the responsibility you've got resting on your shoulders, Doc."

"Tell me about it." He grinned. "Moving on to lighter topics, have you thought any more about my proposal?"

"The blind date?" Craig tensed at the prospect. "I don't need my buddies to set me up with dates."

Matt snorted. "Then why don't you already have a date for the awards dinner?"

Craig looked away. He should have had a date by now, but he hadn't known anyone long enough to be comfortable asking. "Because that isn't the kind of thing you ask someone you just met on Christian Mingle to attend with you."

"Christian Mingle, really?"

"The swipe right app wasn't for me." He chuckled.

"Swipe right app?"

He shrugged. "Don't remember what it was called. But I couldn't get a quality date from it. Too many people on there are only interested in hookups."

"You could always ask Lisa."

"She's a subordinate. Completely inappropriate."

"You could attend together as friends."

"That would require us becoming a bit friendlier. She cannot stand the sight of me."

Matt laughed and pushed through the door, taking a seat in Craig's recently vacated chair, and spinning around in a circle like a toddler. "How about you go out once with this girl Madison wants to set you up with? You'll never have to see her again if the two of you don't hit it off."

Craig grimaced. He could not stand the thought, but Matt was relentless. "Why is this important to you?"

"She's Madison's roommate. As long as she remains single, Madison is going to pester me to find someone for her. You'd like her. I promise. This isn't one of those ugly friend setups. She's a cute girl."

"Sure, she is." He let out a huff. "Fine. Set it up. But I'm only agreeing to one date. If I hate her, I'm bailing."

"You need to stay for the entire dinner. When it's over, you're free to do as you please, but I'm telling you right now, you'll want to see her again. She's not smoking hot like Madison, but she's pretty. And she's sweet."

"Um hmm. We'll see." Craig shook his head. Giving in to his friends' requests never ended well for him. Yet, he was always the sucker who couldn't let people down.

The elevator door opened and Lisa Harper stepped out. When she spotted Matt spinning in the chair, she let out a long-suffering sigh. Even though she was a good five years younger than him, her attitude reminded him of his ninth-grade history teacher. Craig saluted Matt and grinned at Lisa. "You're early."

She made eye contact. "Always." Frowning, she gestured for Matt to remove his rear from the security desk chair.

"That's the thing I like most about you, Lisa. Your punctuality," Craig said.

"I haven't found anything I like about you yet." She deadpanned.

"You will." He tapped his chin. "I'm irresistible."

Chapter Two

Javier opened the back of a sleek black Lincoln Town Car for Alhad, and he slid inside and breathed the scent of supple leather as he reclined into the seat, thankful to escape the cold.

When the driver turned the ignition, the engine roared to life and Feliz Navidad blasted from the speakers.

"Turn off that ruckus." He grimaced. Christmas music was the worst. In any language.

A push of a button heated his seat, warding off the chill. He forced open the panel separating him from Javier. "Another problem has arisen, and I'd like your assistance disposing of it."

"It'll cost you."

"I'm aware. An extra ten grand on top of your fee."

"I want another five percent."

"That's ludicrous."

"Take it or leave it."

"Fine. But only because I don't have the time or inclination to search for someone new to help." He gripped the edge of the seat until his knuckles turned white and bit back a curse. "The reason I came to the backwoods of Pennsylvania was a rumor that a doctor here was close to developing an antidote for my creation. Of course, the government had access to it throughout the testing since it was their lab where I did my research in the mountains of New Mexico, but they seem to have taken the tiny samples I provided and replicated them so that this local yokel could find a way to fight it."

"So what? You'll still get your dinero as long as the auction happens."

"If word gets out that there is an antidote or even that someone is close to developing one, it'll severely hinder the bidding. Which will affect you, too, I might add."

"What do you want me to do about it?"

"Eliminate the doctor and steal his research so I can destroy it or sell it along with my own gift to humanity. It might be best if you burned down the whole lab. I'd prefer to get my hands on the good doctor's work, but I don't want to take the chance that I'll lose my payday by letting his work see the light of day. Your specialty is explosives, right?"

"I'm not a specialist. I pride myself on being a jack of all trades."

Illegal trades. "But you know how to set bombs, am I right?"

"Sure."

"Then blow up the good doctor in his lab, and don't leave anyone connected with him alive."

"That'll draw a lot of attention. Maybe we should just get him to hand over his work. Once you have his work, you can sell it along with Viper-X. Who wouldn't want to buy the antidote along with the weapon?"

"How will we get him to hand it over, pray tell?"

"Figure out who he's closest to. When I take possession of the person he holds most dear, he'll comply with my wishes."

"Fine. Do it your way. Just make sure every trace of it is destroyed or handed over to me."

"Bombing the lab may be the only way to destroy any remnants."

"Then do it." He curled his fingers into fists at his side. "Just be sure to return my case before you get your fool self arrested."

CLARA SCHUMANN'S VIBRANT "PIANO Concerto in A Minor, Op. 7" vibrated off the tile in Sadie's tiny bathroom, blocking out traffic noises from shift change at the hospital. The music rose to a crescendo and she wiped at the steam coating the mirror. She grimaced at the sight of the bright coral lipstick. Too much. When she swiped at it with a tissue, the cheap single-ply stuck to her bottom lip. Dabbing under her eyes with a clean one, she winced and drew a breath in through her teeth when the rough texture brushed against the sensitive skin. Madison brought the cheap sandpaper-like tissues home from the hospital. Sadie preferred the plush ones with lotion in them, and she didn't mind spending extra for them.

A blind date. On Friday the thirteenth? Not that she believed in bad juju or anything, but it wasn't a date she'd choose if it were up to her.

Previous setups had been disasters, so as a rule she avoided them. The last one she'd been on was two years earlier, and it took her two months to get him to stop texting her with random sexist memes.

Tonight, her roommate wanted to go out as a foursome, so Madison was bringing the guy she'd been dating for years, and his friend. An unknown quantity. Sadie had no clue what to expect other than a tedious evening with a stranger. She pressed her sweaty palm down the length of her A-line skirt, removing the wrinkles.

Madison had figured she'd google the guy, so she'd refused to give her a name or a picture so she could prepare herself for the toad she'd be sharing a table with. A colonoscopy would be preferable.

Sadie meandered into her bedroom and glanced at the clock. Maybe there was still time to get out of this. If she called the hospital, she could get someone to call her into work. That would be a believable excuse. Perfectly understandable.

Sadie's foot beat out a rhythm on the hardwood floor as she reached for her cell. Work was preferable to a night spent in the company of a stranger. No question about it.

Madison breezed into the room in a cloud of exotic fragrance. It worked for her. When Sadie tried to wear perfume, it felt like she was trying too hard.

Madison gave her a knowing look and plucked the device from her fingers. "No, you don't." She placed her hands on her hips. "I knew you would try to back out. You were going to get yourself called into work, weren't you?"

"Maybe."

Madison narrowed her eyes and flipped Sadie's phone in the air. "Not happening. I don't ask you for much. Do this one teensy little favor for me, please?"

"You ask me for things all the time." Not five days earlier she'd asked her to cover a twelve-hour shift for her.

Her friend grinned and held the cell to her chest, effectively keeping Sadie from making the call. "Matt made reservations at the Lightstreet Hotel. He and his friend will be here any minute." Madison had met her boyfriend at the University of Pennsylvania where she'd earned her BSN. At the time, he was attending the Perelman School of Medicine where he received a dual degree in microbiology and immunology.

Sadie hadn't met either of them until they took jobs at Geisinger. Matt had since moved on to bigger and better things.

Sadie rolled her eyes. "Fine. I'll go. But if this guy you picked out for me bores me to death, I'm not hanging around so you and Dr. Matt can stare into each other's eyes. I'll sneak into the ladies' room and get the charge nurse to call me into work."

"You have zero sense of adventure. Did it ever occur to you that you might like this guy?"

She laughed. "No. I can honestly say the thought of liking someone you two picked for me never entered my mind. Not even once."

SADIE NOTICED A GUY on the curb thumbing around his cell phone as she and Madison hopped into the backseat of Matt's dark green Subaru Forester. It was roomy inside and the sound system was good, though the opening notes of "Santa Baby" made her cringe and groan inwardly. She loved Christmas, but between Thanksgiving and New Year's, she got a bit warn out with renditions of that and "Let it Snow." Her Spotify playlist was filled with classical music with a few gospel hymns scattered in to remind her of the reason for the season.

The man in the passenger seat turned to face her. "Sadie?"

Her jaw dropped, and she pushed forward to get a better look at the man up front. Craig Malone was her date. This couldn't be happening. He'd teased her mercilessly through her awkward skinny phase, the braces, and even the lisp she'd suffered from in first and second grade before working with the speech therapist. Craig had been their next-door neighbor and her brother's best friend. The source of her biggest crush and most painful heartbreak.

Instead of voicing her thoughts, she forced a smile. "Hi, Craig. Long time no see."

"What's it been? Five years?"

"Ten."

"Nah. I was at your graduation party."

"High school graduation. That was before college."

"Your brother said you're a nurse now. I never pictured you in a job like that."

"Nobody did." Except her. She always knew she wanted a career that would allow her to help people. Registered nurse was the path she'd taken to help her reach that goal.

Craig smacked the headrest and raised his eyebrows in Madison's direction. "You should've seen her back then. A tiny butterfly flitting all over the place. Couldn't pin her down."

"I'm not sure you're remembering high school."

"Nah. Picturing you in your tutu back in ... what was it? Third-grade recital?"

"I believe that was first grade. The only year I took ballet."

"You should've stuck with it. Probably missed your calling."

Great. She was going on a date with someone who had visions of her dressed as a teeny tiny sugarplum. No wonder he never noticed her in high school. The time she'd asked him to accompany her to the Sadie Hawkins dance, he'd laughed. Yes. Laughed. Right in her face. Sucking in a sharp breath, she tried to organize her thoughts and come up with an excuse to cut out of this date early.

Matt pulled into a parking spot outside of the restaurant and Craig hopped out and reached for their door. Madison squeezed Sadie's arm. "You okay?" She whispered the question.

"You really should've let me see a picture or given me his name." Sadie spoke under her breath, but it didn't keep Matt from giving her a sideways glance before joining Craig on the sidewalk.

"I'm getting that. Please try to have fun tonight. Forget him."

Sadie grimaced. How was she supposed to manage that? Sitting across from Craig Malone. She slipped out of the vehicle after Madison. Her arm brushed against Craig, who closed the door behind her before falling into step beside her.

"You look fantastic." His smile told her his compliment was genuine, but it was tough to reciprocate.

"Thanks. What are you doing in the area? Last I heard, you were stationed in Hawaii."

"I'm back. Working for the government."

"Doing what?"

"That's classified."

"Very funny."

Matt walked backwards. "Craig works with me. And as you know, what I do is classified."

There was a disconnect somewhere in Sadie's brain. There was no way she could connect the work Matt did with Craig's experience as a Navy SEAL. She didn't know much about Matt's work, but she'd always assumed it was health-care related despite the secrecy surrounding his research.

Chapter Three

The aroma of cinnamon and apples mingled with the heady scent of pine in the foyer of the historic building currently decorated with festive lights and greenery. Definitely smelled like Christmas. The clatter of dishes contrasted with the gentle rhythms of "I'll Be Home for Christmas" playing in the background. Her shoulders relaxed, and she smiled, her inner Grinch melting away as they reached their table. She'd make the most of the date she'd longed for back when she was a girl. It couldn't hurt to enjoy Craig's company. It'd be easier if he'd stop teasing her though.

Craig pulled out a chair for her and helped her scoot in before taking his seat beside her at the round table where they'd been seated. She looked up at the specials on the board. Three different types of steak stared down at her.

"I'm hungry enough for two steaks. Took so long for

Matt to drive us here, I thought I'd have to gnaw off my arm. He drives slower than a grandma."

"Whose grandma?" She winked. "Yours is a lead foot."

Chuckling, he shifted his attention to the server as she approached. He ordered an appetizer platter for all of them to share, and both women ordered filet mignon with vegetables and rice on the side, while the men ordered prime rib and baked potatoes.

"Back to the lead-footed grandmother. I'd like to hear more about this phenomenon." Matt raised a brow.

Craig took a sip of water and shook his head. "We shouldn't have let her keep her car when she insisted on moving into the assisted living facility. She's a menace to everyone on and off the road."

Sadie laughed as she spread the serviette across her lap. "She absolutely is."

As she reached for a potato skin, her hand brushed Craig's, and the smile he gave her sent shivers down her spine and warmed her all the way to her toes. Too bad it was just one date. When she arrived back home tonight, she would forget any fantasy of a relationship with the boy next door. Like Cinderella after the ball, she would hurry home and try to forget him. She curled her fingers into the folds of her cloth napkin until they ached from the pressure. There would be no return of her prince. He was off-limits. Exploring a relationship with him wasn't worth the repeat heartache.

WHEN THEY ARRIVED AT the girls' place, Craig let himself out and held the door for Sadie, while Matt slipped out and did the same for Madison. The doors clicked shut and Craig ran a hand along the smooth surface of the SUV. He might get himself a Forester for his next vehicle.

They escorted the ladies up the single flight of stairs to their apartment.

"Do you guys want to come in for a coffee?" Madison smiled coquettishly.

Matt took her hand and rubbed it with his thumb. "Next time. I have an early day tomorrow."

She stuck her bottom lip out in what Craig assumed was supposed to be a sexy pout, but looked more like a petulant child to him. He kept his facial features schooled, but struggled to keep from rolling his eyes. Sadie rescued him from the scene playing out. "Tonight was nice." She lifted onto her tiptoes and kissed his cheek. He shut his eyes for a second and reveled in the sensation of her lips against his skin.

"It was. I'm glad you were the blind date. I was dreading this until I saw you tonight."

"I'm glad I wasn't a disappointment." Her smile twisted his guts, but he blinked and tamped down the sensation. Nobody was more off-limits than Brian's sister.

"It was good to see you, Sadie."

"You too."

Matt wrapped up his goodbye, and they descended the stairs and strolled back to their vehicle.

Once they were inside, Craig swiveled to face Matt and rapped his knuckles on the dash. "Dude, you blindsided me."

"What? I didn't know you two had a history." Matt turned up the volume on the radio and pulled out into traffic.

Craig flipped the volume back off. "She's my best friend's sister. Off-limits. Besides, she's way too young for me." But Sadie hadn't looked young in that skirt and those heels. Heaven help him, she was not the girl he remembered.

"You've never dated someone a few years younger?"

"Not someone who was like a sister to me. I remember her in pigtails and whistling through the gap between her two front teeth. I need to keep that image of her in my brain."

"You might want to open your eyes. Sadie is a grown woman. If I wasn't dating Madison, I'd definitely take her out. Not only is she gorgeous, she's compassionate, generous, witty, and intelligent. There aren't too many women out there who have so much going for them."

"Believe me, I know. I've tried to find a decent girl to settle down with, but either they want no part in my career choice, or they're only interested in me because of it, like it's some kind of badge of honor for them to say they had a fling with a former SEAL."

"Who doesn't enjoy a fling with an attractive woman?"

"I've moved on from shallow relationships. I'd rather be alone than have a series of one-night stands."

"I never had women throwing themselves at me, but I doubt I'd have the power to say no."

Craig shook his head. His friend didn't know how

good he had it with his girlfriend.

"Don't let Madison hear you talk like that."

"Trust me, I won't."

"Moving on from the topic of girls. With the threat of a pending sale looming, Washington wants your antidote. They want countermeasures put in place yesterday."

"We're working on it."

"Might call for a few long nights and some time away from dates with your girl."

"She understands that."

"Glad you found someone like her, but we can't all be so lucky. I'm destined to be single."

"Don't be ridiculous." Matt shook his head, then returned his focus to the road. "Tonight you had dinner with a woman who may not be perfect, but she may just be perfect for you. Give it a chance."

"I don't know. Too risky."

"Some things are worth the risk." Matt pulled into a spot in front of Craig's Airbnb rental. He clasped him on the shoulder. "It's time to think about settling down. Find a girl. Buy a house. Unless you plan to stay in short-term housing for the duration of your time in Pennsylvania?"

"I don't know. I'm kind of hoping we'll finish up soon, and they'll send me some place else."

"That might be why you can't find a nice girl to settle down with. Few want to commit to a guy who can't even commit to a place to call home for more than a couple of months at a time."

Matt's words echoed through his brain as he dug out

his keys and let himself in. The words were painfully true.

THE FOLLOWING MORNING, SADIE dressed in her scrubs then went to the kitchen where Madison sat with the morning paper spread out in front of her. Madison munched on an iced cinnamon Pop-Tart. Sadie refrained from pointing out all the reasons why her friend's breakfast choice wasn't ideal as she poured coffee into her own mug and inhaled the rich aroma of her favorite French roast. After grabbing a cutting board, she took fresh fruit and cottage cheese from the refrigerator to prepare her own morning meal.

She arranged a peach on the cutting board and gripped the cool handle of their chef's knife, drawing it from the holder. Her hold on the handle stiffened when she saw a man standing near the bank, looking up at their window. A shiver slid down her spine. "Did you notice that guy standing near the bank?"

"What guy?" Madison caught some crumbs in a napkin and shook it onto her plate.

"Some dude in running gear." Sadie turned back to her task, swiftly slicing through the peach. "I feel like I should know him from somewhere. And I'm pretty sure he was hanging around last night when Matt picked us up."

"Maybe he's new to the area." Madison sipped from her mug.

Sadie put her breakfast into a bowl and carried it to the table. "I guess that's possible."

"You're being paranoid. Wasn't that house over by the hospital for sale? Maybe he bought it. If he works at the hospital, that would explain why he looks familiar."

"I can't imagine anyone paying that much for a house on a quarter acre of land when you can drive twenty minutes in any direction and get three times the land and twice the house for the same price." Sadie took a bite of peaches and cottage cheese. Closing her eyes, she savored the flavor. Cool, sweet goodness.

"A doctor working at the hospital might be willing to pay more. Us nurses can't afford it."

"Says the girl who snagged herself a doctor and will soon leave me to fend for myself. Besides, we make plenty. I have no complaints."

"Being close does make it easier when you get called into work." Madison brushed the crumbs from the table into her hand and deposited them in the trash can.

Sadie savored the sweetness of the peaches before responding. "Sometimes I wish we lived farther so they'd be less apt to call us first."

"Yeah. I don't know if that would help. They call Linda in and she lives all the way out in Red Rock." Madison rose to her feet and twisted her blond locks into a bun and secured it with the bobby pins stashed in her pocket.

"True."

"You'd better finish up. We need to get on the road."

"We could walk today. It's not supposed to get too cold."

"No thanks. I don't plan on walking home at midnight if we wind up working overtime again."

"Fair enough." It wasn't out of the realm of possibilities. They were asked to work late more often than not.

Chapter Four

Sadie's feet ached by midday. Lunch break arrived, and she hustled through the sterile white hallway toward the cafeteria, her face buried in her cell phone checking her recent texts from her brother, Brian. Apparently, Craig found it amusing that they'd been setup on a blind date together and immediately shared the news with her brother, who also saw the hilarity of the situation. Her teeth clenched and her insides burned thinking about them having fun at her expense. Again.

Well, she'd given it a chance. She'd enjoyed a nice evening with Craig. But a repeat performance wasn't going to happen. He hadn't asked. And if he had, she would've declined without hesitation. No sense in enduring the embarrassment of them talking about her behind her back. She looked up to avoid a collision, and her gaze slammed into familiar olive-green eyes. Warmth flooded her face and neck. A hint of a scent unique to him wafted toward her, and her stomach betrayed her with a little flip of excitement. "What are you doing here?"

Craig grinned and stopped in front of her, blocking her path. "What kind of welcome is that, sunshine?"

"Sunshine?"

"I was trying it on for size. Isn't that what your dad used to call you?"

"You are so not him."

"Nevertheless, I think I like it."

"Why are you here?"

"Can't a guy walk the corridors of a hospital without getting questioned by the staff?"

She put a hand on her waist and waited for an answer.

"We have a tip that a guy we're looking for was brought in the other night after a multi-car accident involving a bus. Gave a fake name to police at the scene, but facial recognition was run on the officer's dash cam footage, and we think it's him."

"Him who?"

"Wouldn't you like to know, sweetheart?"

"Stop it with the nicknames. I'm Sadie. I've always been Sadie. I'll always be Sadie."

"Okay, Sadie. The guy's a doctor, but he's not the Mr. Nice Guy type. He created something bad and then absconded with it. We need to take him into custody before he follows through with some pretty awful plans."

"I think you can probably be a bit more specific."

"Wish I could, but..."

"It's classified."

"Yep."

"I was here when the victims from the crash were brought in. Maybe I can help. Do you have a picture of the man?"

"Sure. Can we go somewhere to talk?"

"I was headed to the cafeteria to get a salad. Care to join me?"

"Like a second date?"

"No. Like a federal official wanting information from a witness."

He settled into step beside her as they neared the cafeteria. "Did you just shoot me down?"

"I do believe I did. Yes." Dishes clattered in the distance, and the faint odor of garlic made her stomach growl.

SADIE TOOK A SEAT at a round table in the corner, and Craig chose the seat beside her that gave him the best view of the room.

As she ate her salad, he scanned the area, locating the exits and studying the faces of the patrons. When she pushed away her salad, he handed her his cell. "Take a look at that guy. Recognize him?"

She folded her arms across her chest. "What about patient confidentiality? I don't want to breach it."

Leaning closer to her, he asked, "Are you going to make me get a warrant?"

The corner of her lips nudged upward in a half smile.

"I may do that. Unless you can show me some identification so I know you really work for the government. If I'm going to breach this guy's rights, I'll need a good reason."

"I can get the warrant, Sadie. It won't be hard." Craig rapped his knuckles on the smooth tabletop.

"Then do that. I'm sure the paperwork will have the name of the agency you're working for stamped all over it."

Sucking in a deep breath of coffee-laden air, he flipped open his credentials, letting her inspect them.

"Homeland Security? Never would've pegged you for the type. Do you wear a nondescript suit and drive a nondescript dark-colored SUV?"

Craig gestured down to his jeans and polo shirt. "What do you think?"

"I think I forced your hand, and you told me who you work for."

Stuffing his credentials back into his pocket, he studied her a moment, then grinned. She was different. No doubt about it. This new and improved model of the girl next door was sassy with a touch of belligerence, but she could also be helpful. If she chose to be.

She wiped the sweat from her water bottle. "He checked in under the name Adam Smith."

"Not terribly original, huh?" He chuckled.

"The bad news is that he was discharged the following morning. His wounds weren't severe enough to need immediate intervention, so he was referred to see his regular practitioner for further care."

"You've got to be kidding me." He shoved his phone back into his pocket.

"I have more news."

"What's that?"

"I think a friend of his has been following me."

Craig's eyes widened, and he stared at her. "Following you?" If this guy was following Sadie, he'd just made the whole operation personal. Though it was far more likely he was interested in Matt's girlfriend.

"Either me or Madison. I've seen him on the street by our apartment a few times. He looked familiar, but I couldn't place where I'd seen him before until you showed me the other guy's photo. He was hanging around Adam Smith's room the entire time he was here."

"And you've seen him near your place?"

"He was on the street by our house when Matt swung by to pick us up last night. I saw him again this morning by the bank across the street from our place, staring up at our window."

"You didn't think that was suspicious?"

"I did, yes. I mentioned it to Madison. She suggested I was being paranoid, so I let it go."

"You weren't, but it's most likely her he's following. This guy may have a vested interest in Matt's work."

"Why? What's Matt working on?"

"That's—"

"Classified." She lifted the plastic container with the remainder of her salad in it and deposited it in a nearby trash bin. "Well, I hope you find him."

Craig dug out a business card and scribbled his personal cell number across the back before handing it to her. "Call if you see him again. Or if you decide to take me up on that second date."

SADIE SQUIRMED UNDER MADISON'S stare for a full thirty seconds before striding from the room. Her friend followed. "Why won't you call him? He wouldn't have given you his number if he didn't want to see you again."

"Were you listening to a word I said? He came by to talk about a patient, not about what a wonderful time he had with me at dinner. His offer of a second date was an afterthought. He probably thought I'd be more likely to call him with more information if I thought he had some interest in me." She fiddled with her smart watch.

"Is he right?" Madison narrowed her eyes.

"No. Of course not." She plopped down on the sofa and pulled a plush Sherpa throw over her lap, reveling in the added warmth. "I would help him because it's the right thing to do. Those two guys sound like creeps. Although, a bad doctor who does bad things doesn't tell me too much about what is really going on. I guess the second guy is his muscle? I don't know."

"From what I gather, Matt's been working on something to combat a bio-terrorist attack. If these guys want to get a hold of it, they are definitely creeps."

Sadie sat up straight. "How do you know what Matt's working on? Isn't it supposed to be classified?"

Madison tilted her head to the side. "I overheard a

phone call with his boss."

"Ah." She raised a brow. "Eavesdropping?"

"I might've been." Madison shrugged, then she rubbed the back of her neck and made eye contact. "Look, I'm sorry I didn't take you seriously when you warned me about that runner guy. Does Craig honestly think he's stalking me?"

"He wants to get to Matt, and you may be the best way for him to do that."

"So, he's following me to get to Matt?" Her spine stiffened.

"He didn't say, but it could even mean he'd kidnap you to get Matt to turn over his work. I mean that's how it happens in books and movies, right?"

Madison's face paled, and she took a step backward. "You can't be serious. How are you so nonchalant about all this?"

"I'm not. It's just that I can't picture Craig doing the kind of serious work that would involve terrorist threats. It's so at odds with the kid I knew, but he's a grown man now. I need to get used to who he is now." Sadie jumped to her feet and strode to the window where she pushed aside the curtains just enough so that she could see out. A chill crawled up her spine. "Mr. Thug is all too real, and he's back. I'm calling Craig."

Chapter Five

The drive to Sadie's place was less than five minutes from where he was staying, but knowing that a traitor was standing mere feet from her abode made his insides churn. He'd called it in, so local cops should already be there. She would be safe. It wasn't her he was after. Matt was the target. Somehow that didn't ease his worry.

After running a red light and rolling a few stop signs, he arrived outside the gray stone building. A look in every direction told him nobody lurked nearby other than a police car with lights flashing and sirens screaming over in the bank parking lot. He swiftly crossed to the waiting officer, showed him his identification, and asked if he'd apprehended the suspect. No such luck. He'd been gone when they'd arrived on the scene. He headed to the front door and prayed the guy hadn't made it inside. He withdrew his Glock from its holster, its weight comforting, as he pushed the outer door open and hit the buzzer for the second-floor apartment. Madison answered with a shaky voice. "Craig?"

"Yeah. It's me." His heart hammered against his chest with the thought that she could be in danger.

She buzzed him in, and he raced up the stairs, his feet pounding on the treads. Before taking the time to greet the two women, he cleared the apartment to make sure the guy hadn't entered and forced them to act normally. Once he was sure it was safe, he threw his arms open for Sadie to step into. She hesitated at first, but then threw herself into his embrace, clutching him with the same ferocity she had that time in middle school when she'd been jumped by a group of girls, and he'd broken it up. Her body trembled beneath his touch, and his throat tightened, cutting off the words he wished to speak. Words that would tell her he'd protect her from this threat and any other. Keeping her safe had always been a priority. And despite years apart, that hadn't changed.

When she took a step back, he cleared his throat. "He got away."

"We saw him cut across toward the hospital. It's shift change for a lot of the nurses, so he probably managed to blend with the crowd. I doubt you'll be able to find him now."

"I'm not leaving the two of you alone until we do."

Madison tilted her head. "Aren't you supposed to be working at the lab? Protecting Matt's research?"

"I am. Yes." He lifted his phone from his pocket. "But I'm not the only agent working for Homeland Security. I'll get one of my team out to the lab. I'm sticking with you two. Something tells me your friend will be back."

Sadie frowned and pointed out the window. "Your vehicle will give you away. He'll know there's a fed here. That's bound to keep him away."

"That's what we want."

"That won't help you catch him."

"But it'll keep you two safe."

CRAIG AND MADISON FEASTED on takeout from Tri Pi in Bloomsburg, courtesy of Grub Hub, while Sadie picked at her spinach salad. It was a healthier option. And the grilled chicken and raspberry vinaigrette dressing gave it a nice tangy flavor, but the aroma of garlic knots filled the entire apartment, making her mouth water. Craig took one, dipped it in sauce and gathered up some extra garlic and set it beside her salad. How could he possibly know how much she wanted that?

"You always loved garlic bread, so I can only imagine you like these just as much."

She hesitated. It wasn't healthy. She shouldn't eat it, but carbs were her undoing. "I try to eat healthier these days."

"That's good, but an occasional splurge won't hurt you. Will it?"

A tiny smile played at the corners of her lips. "I suppose not." She lifted the delectable treat to her lips and savored her first bite of buttery deliciousness, closing her eyes as she chewed. Yum. Garlicky goodness.

Craig smiled. "You have a look of sheer ecstasy on your face."

"Do not."

"Yes." Madison laughed and pointed to her. "Yes, you do."

"We need to figure out what we're going to do about stalker dude." Sadie set her food down and wiped her fingers with a flimsy paper napkin.

"Stalker dude?" Craig choked on his water.

"That's what I've been calling him in my head."

"Why not make up a name?" he asked.

"Just as easy to call him stalker dude or Mr. Thug." She frowned. "Now, the question remains, what are we going to do about him?"

"We're not going to do anything other than provide a security presence to keep the two of you safe."

"But you can't follow us around at work. It would be smarter to set him up, so he can think you're gone. He'll try again to get to us. When that happens, you can get him instead."

"I don't like the idea of using you as bait, Sadie."

"But if it works, we can all go back to our normal routines." It would work, but there was no sense in belaboring the point. He'd made up his mind. And really, was that what she wanted? Her old version of normal. In the few days Craig had been back, something between them had changed. He still teased her, but there was a new feel to their banter. It was different somehow. She wanted to be safe, but she wasn't sure how she felt about returning to life without Craig.

CRAIG SPUN ONE OF the tiny Christmas balls on the miniature Christmas tree that sat on one of Madison and Sadie's end tables. His eyeballs felt like sandpaper after he'd spent most of the night on their couch keeping guard. He lifted a snowflake off the tree and ran his finger along the soft velvety surface. The tree was the only nod to the holiday present in their apartment. His phone buzzed in his pocket, so he withdrew it and excused himself to answer a call from his boss. Quentin Finnegan was fast becoming a friend. Adopted as a child, his Irish surname was at odds with his dark coloring.

"Leaving here is a terrible idea. We can't leave these young women unprotected." His shoulders tensed and his grip tightened on his cell.

"Our priority is Dr. Wright's antidote. You need to be there. We can get local police to handle security for the girls."

"You don't understand the situation here." He wasn't leaving Sadie alone. It wasn't safe. He glanced into the other room and made eye contact with her.

"Excuse me?" There was a hard edge to Quentin's voice.

Craig breathed deep and slow and relaxed his shoulders, all in an effort to soften his tone of voice. "This town is tiny. They don't have the resources to offer protection."

"Then take them with you, but I want you at the lab.

ASAP."

Furrows formed in his forehead. "Sir—." The line went dead. He clenched his fist at his side. Bringing the ladies into a secure facility wasn't an option. His boss knew that good and well. He was being difficult. It was true. Craig's job was to protect the project. But how could he leave Brian's little sister without a safety net? He'd call Brian. No doubt he'd be here before day's end. Not a chance he'd let Sadie's life be in danger without risking his own life to protect her.

He texted Brian to call him and headed back into the living room where he would need to pretend nothing had changed, when the truth was everything had changed.

Chapter Six

The buzzer sounded with its usual grating noise, and Sadie darted her gaze between Madison and Craig. "Expecting anyone?"

Craig squirmed in his seat, rubbing his palms on his slacks.

Madison hurried to the intercom to find out who was there. It would be so much better if they had video so they could see who was down there.

"Can I help you?" Madison asked.

"It's Brian. For Sadie."

Maddie hit the button to buzz him in. "Your brother is here. Doesn't he live hours from here?"

"Two and a half hours to be precise." Her eye twitched. Craig was responsible. No question about it.

"And he didn't warn you he was coming? What if you hadn't been home?"

Craig got to his feet, and Sadie charged, jabbing him

in the chest with her index finger. "You did this, didn't you?"

"I had to." He avoided eye contact with her, his gaze flicking to the door.

A hand flew to her hip, and she tapped her foot. "The last thing I need is my brother here to protect me."

A knock on their apartment door had Madison crossing the room. She gave Sadie a stern look. "Play nice."

Brian greeted Sadie with a huge grin before lifting her in a bear hug that stole the air from her lungs. Brian's cologne assaulted her senses, and she twisted to escape its overpowering onslaught. Her brother's gregarious personality, though genuine, always baffled Sadie. How had they both come from the same parents? She preferred to hide in a corner with a book rather than socialize. He was the lead in the school play, played in a local band, and quarterbacked the football team. If he wasn't the center of attention, he wasn't happy.

The past few years he'd been working as a cop in the town they'd grown up in outside of Philadelphia. Ridley Township. The police drove in red cars that intimidated neighboring troublemakers. Technically, their address had been Swarthmore, but as her uncle liked to say: 'If your place gets robbed, and it will, what police station are you calling?' It wasn't true. Their house hadn't been robbed, and hopefully never would be, but if trouble ever happened, they would call the Ridley P.D. So, despite their fancy zip code, they were still Ridley kids. Currently, Brian had a house in the Folsom section, and he had no desire to leave the town where they'd been raised.

Sadie rolled her eyes. "Craig told you about our stalker." It was a statement, not a question. Not that she minded too much. Having someone care enough to drop everything and drive all that way for her felt good. Every girl should have a brother like him.

He shook his head. "Why didn't you tell me?"

She sighed. "I didn't want you dropping everything to drive out here and play the role of hero. We're fine. Madison and I can take care of ourselves."

"Speak for yourself. I, for one, am happy to see your brother. If Craig has to go back to the lab, we need someone willing to look out for us."

"We're strong, capable women. We do not need men to protect us."

"Have you taken a good look at that guy that's been hanging around? He has to be at least six foot two, and his muscles have muscles."

Sadie shrugged. "We spend most of our time at the hospital. He isn't going to bother us there."

"I hope you're right, but I don't mind the extra security."

"How did you get the time off work?"

"I told Dad you were in danger, and he sent me straight away."

She closed her eyes. Having the chief of police for a father could at times be a good thing, but sometimes it posed more of a headache than a benefit. "Dad knows, too. Great. Just fabulous." She faced Craig. "You'll pay for this."

Sadie pivoted on her heel and ducked into her bedroom to give herself a moment to think.

CRAIG STOOD AND RAKED his fingers through his hair. "That could've gone better."

"Why didn't you warn her you were calling me?" Brian shifted his weight.

A smile tipped his lips. "Who knows? I guess I'm a glutton for punishment. That sister of yours has fire in her veins."

"Don't get any ideas, buddy."

"Just saying."

"She's off-limits."

"I need to get going. You have things under control here?"

Brian nodded. "Sadie will calm down after she takes a few minutes to get used to the idea that I'm sticking around a while. She loves me, and if I know her at all, then I'd say she's probably relieved that I'm here, but doesn't want to admit to needing anyone."

Madison chuckled. "Sounds about right." She headed to the window overlooking the street. "Hey, Craig."

"Yeah?"

"He's back."

Peering outside, he spotted the joker in a car just a few spots behind his own. "I'm taking your Explorer, Brian. Keys? I imagine he's figured out what I'm driving by now. Yours will give me the element of surprise." He held out his hand and Brian deposited them in his palm.

"You want me to come with?"

"Better one of us stays here in case I lose him."

Craig took the stairs two at a time, jumping the bottom three to pick up an extra second. When he emerged from the building, the thug they'd seen from inside was nowhere to be found. His car was gone, too. Must've noticed them watching him from the window. Hoping to catch the wayward chemist, he jumped into Brian's Ford Explorer and took off, pressing the accelerator hard to the floor. Before he made it off the street, the Explorer jerked and jumped as an explosion shook the area.

In his rearview mirror, he saw what Sadie would refer to as his nondescript government-issued SUV engulfed by flames. Thank the Lord he wasn't in it. He bowed his head in gratitude after he pulled to the curb. His death had been Alhad Sharma's plan. Or his cohort's plan. Either way, he'd come far too close to being barbecued alive.

He'd anticipated this kind of thing when he became a Navy SEAL. Yet, when he joined Homeland Security, he'd expected things to be less drama-filled. Quieter. Not so.

Another prayer of gratitude fell off his lips as he climbed from Brian's SUV and walked over to his own. Cheated death again. Unbelievable.

SADIE WAS AT HER bedroom window watching the street

when a deafening explosion shattered the quiet, and she gaped down at Craig's SUV bursting into flames. She prayed he wasn't in it, then dashed into the living room where she found Brian calming Madison.

Sadie locked eyes with her brother. "Take care of her. I need to check on Craig. If he was in his car..." She shook her head.

"He wasn't. He took my car," Brian said.

Sadie darted from the apartment, down the stairs, and out the door. The acrid smell of burnt rubber stung her nostrils when she inhaled.

Craig stood beside the charred remains of his vehicle, batting away thick clouds of black smoke, but he looked unscathed.

Her whole body trembled in relief. She paused for two beats, then flung herself into his arms. "Thank heaven you're all right. When I saw your car..."

"Shh. I'm all right. Everything's okay." He rubbed circles on her back.

Brian appeared beside them.

She stepped back, heat rushing into her face despite the frigid air. She rarely expressed herself, but she had difficulty containing herself when she did.

Brian stood to the side; his head tilted as he studied her.

"I was worried. Craig's like family." Sirens sounded in the distance.

"Okay." Brian motioned to the crowd forming around them.

They were surrounded by people. They must've come

from the neighboring residences and businesses. Her face warmed and she winced at her uncharacteristic behavior. "I'm going to go back inside and check on my roommate." Sirens punctuated her words, but Madison didn't give her the chance to move. She barreled through the front door and settled herself between Sadie and Brian.

A firetruck arrived with lights flashing. Men hopped from the truck, pulled the hose free, and shot water at the burning vehicle.

Brian grasped Craig's shoulder. "You okay?"

His calm question contrasted with Sadie's overreaction, making Sadie seem even more out of control. She hated over-the-top displays of emotion, but after seeing his car explode, the sight of him unharmed was such a relief. Craig came up behind her and placed his hand on the small of her back, steering her toward the back of the building. When they were out of earshot of the others, he pulled her in for a hug. "I think it's sweet that you were worried about me. Stop stressing over how other people see you."

She hesitated, unsure how to respond. How did he know what was running through her head?

He clasped her hand, keeping her in place. "I want that second date, Sadie. What your brother thinks about it doesn't matter one iota to me anymore."

"It's probably a bad idea."

"A terrible one." He grinned. "But let's do it anyway. Tomorrow night? What time does your shift end?"

"Tomorrow's Wednesday, right?"

"All day."

"My shift is supposed to end at seven, but that doesn't mean it will."

"In that case, we'll call it a tentative date, provided you don't have to stay. I'll pick you up at eight unless I hear from you otherwise."

Two police cars pulled up. An ambulance joined them less than a minute later. Craig gave her one last look, then strode back to where Brian stood speaking with an officer. Before she knew it, he disappeared into her brother's car while she absorbed the weight of their conversation. As she replayed his words 'I want that second date,' she grinned. Craig asked her out. And she'd accepted. A poor idea, indeed, but that wouldn't stop her from going.

JAVIER STARED OUT THE loft window of the old barn where he was holed up. The faint musky aroma from the livestock that had once inhabited the place lingered, but it offered a view of the commotion he'd caused when his device detonated. If the cops were smart, they'd think to look for him here. Leaning back against a hay bale, a smug smile slowly crept across his face. Plenty of nooks and crannies where he could conceal himself if they ventured over.

His target had messed up his plans when he'd switched cars, but all was not lost. It would serve as a wakeup call for his doctor friend. Dr. Matthew Wright would recognize the seriousness of the situation when Javier took what mattered the most. Choosing proved difficult. The man seemed partial to the tall blonde, but his mother was a valid option. In fact, after observing the man with his sweet madre, Javier thought she might be the greater love in the good doctor's life. Only time would tell. But he didn't have too much of that left. So, if he could grab one or both of the girls, he would. The mom could serve as his backup plan if he wouldn't hand over his work product.

His boss wasn't thinking clearly. He could have backup copies on the cloud of all his research, and he could've shared it with someone. There might be samples that were put in a safe place. Even if he managed to get the work from him, it didn't mean the antidote wouldn't be developed. It might take longer if the lab was destroyed, but unless they could find a way to guarantee that Dr. Wright gave them everything, it could still be viable even after they stole it.

Chapter Seven

Craig arrived and rode the elevator to the lab where he gowned up and entered Matt's work area. The hum of fluorescent lights was the only sound in the space where Matt bent over a specimen. "We need to get a new lab up and running. Somewhere else where you can finish your work."

"That could take months. This needs to be done now. I'm not going anywhere."

"They blew up my vehicle."

"I know, Madison called. That's craziness."

"Yes. It is." Craig fixed Matt with a hard stare. "What happens when they do the same thing to the lab?"

"They wouldn't. This building is full of other people and businesses. There is the hospital billing department, and a bio-medical testing facility."

"Exactly."

"You're saying if I don't relocate, I'm putting everyone

else in danger."

Craig made a weighing motion with his hands. "It wouldn't necessarily be *you* putting them in danger, but you may have the chance to minimize that risk. You should take it."

"Do you think they can set up a lab quickly? Like within twenty-four hours instead of a few months?"

"I don't know what half of the stuff in here is let alone what it does, but I'll get you on the line with someone who speaks geek, and we'll get you whatever you need."

"Okay. I'll agree to move, but not if it's going to back up my timeline."

"Understood." Craig let out a breath. "Believe me when I tell you, Homeland Security doesn't want the delay any more than you do."

A few calls later, they had made arrangements to move the entire operation to a government lab in Philadelphia located in center city. It could be ready by morning. Now he needed to get Sadie and Madison to accept protection, too. What Sadie didn't know wouldn't hurt her. He'd arrange things with Brian, and they could take it from there. And Matt could convince Madison.

If they could keep from being followed, Matt could complete his work and everyone should be safe once again. Of course, they would still need to apprehend the criminals responsible for the theft in New Mexico and the explosion in Danville, but that didn't fall into his job description. He was basically a glorified bodyguard ... well, not so much a body, as a project guard. He needed to protect Matt's work product. The US government would be far less concerned over Matt's death than it would be his work falling into the hands of their enemies. Understandable, maybe, but not the most comforting thought.

SADIE WENT INTO THE break room and breathed in the alluring aroma of coffee. She grabbed a cup and set up the Keurig. Danielle was lounging in a chair at a circular table, staring at her phone.

"Did you see this?"

"See what?" Sadie asked.

"That seven-year-old boy that was brought in over the weekend. He's been moved out of PICU to a regular room."

She smiled. When he'd been brought in, she wasn't sure he'd get through surgery, much less leave the Pediatric Intensive Care Unit so quickly. The kid was a fighter.

"The family credits God and prayer for his miraculous recovery. To listen to them tell the story, you'd think all the doctors and nurses just stood around lollygagging while God waved his magic wand."

"Hasn't anyone ever told you God works through everyday men and women?" Sadie leaned back in her chair and looked at the ceiling, counting to three. She got sick of people like her coworker belittling Christians for putting their faith in God.

"How can you believe in something you can't see? You

have a Bachelor of Science in nursing. Science. I believe in science. So should you."

"Science is all about testing theories, and God is the only theory I ever tested that never let me down. Does gravity make sense to you? You can't see it. What about the air you breathe? It isn't visible either. God may not be visible, but I can feel Him as clearly as I can see you."

"Don't be ridiculous."

"What's truly ridiculous is for you to presume God isn't as real as gravity or oxygen. I know my Savior as intimately as I know the air I breathe." She pointed to her chest. "He's a constant presence with me. I could no more deny Him than I can deny myself my next breath." With that, she walked out of the break room without bothering to fill her cup. She might not have the power to change people's beliefs, but she'd never listen to them rant against hers without a response. Praise the Lord that child had a family who was praying for him. She'd been praying as well. And she absolutely believed in the power of prayer.

Her phone buzzed with an incoming text. It was from Brian.

Brian: Need to see you. New development.

Sadie: Meet me outside of the ED. I could use some fresh air.

The last time she'd seen her brother, he was helping the carpenters remove the extra chairs that had been brought into the waiting room for family and friends when they'd had that code black. At least it stopped him from hovering. His continual hovering had already gotten the attention of the charge nurse, and she'd had to explain the situation. The woman would allow it for the night as long as Brian stayed far enough away to keep from overhearing confidential patient details, but she planned to seek counsel from the higher-ups on whether it was advisable that Sadie take a leave of absence rather than have a 'bodyguard' with her at work. There was no doubt in Sadie's mind that she'd be temporarily dismissed rather than given an accommodation. And if Danielle reported her for talking about God in the break room, she might be given the permanent boot. She chuckled to herself as she walked out the emergency department doors and breathed in fumes from a nearby ambulance. So much for fresh air.

Brian joined her less than a minute later. "We need to leave town."

"Why?"

"Because it'll be easier on Homeland Security if we're all in one place. They're moving Matt's lab, and they want us to either find somewhere to vacation where nobody knows us, or we can stay close to where Matt's going."

"And where is that?"

"They'll tell us on the way. Don't want to take any chance we'll tell anybody."

"And Madison?"

"She's with Matt and Craig. They picked her up at your place twenty minutes ago."

"I have another three hours remaining on my shift." And then Craig was supposed to pick her up for their date. Guess that wasn't happening.

"Craig's boss already called your boss."

"I'm not comfortable leaving them shorthanded."

"You won't be. That was taken care of, too."

"You knew about all this before now."

He shook his head. "I didn't, but Craig did. He waited until the last possible moment to spring it on us. Security protocols."

CRAIG REACHED FOR HIS phone for the umpteenth time in the past half hour. Brian should've confirmed that he and Sadie were on the road by now. They would drive down in Sadie's car and switch vehicles halfway. He'd arranged for them to pick up a rental in Allentown. That way if anyone had installed a tracker on her car it would lead them to the wrong place.

When they called from their rental, he'd give them their destination address. He hated all the secrecy, but listening devices were so small these days they could be anywhere. The best way to keep all of them and the antidote safe was to compartmentalize and only disseminate information as needed. He had no doubt this process was aggravating Sadie, but it couldn't be helped.

His phone rang, and he snatched it up on the first ring. "It's about time, Brian."

"Not Brian."

"Oh. You called from his phone."

"He made me leave mine in my purse back at my

apartment. Where are we going?"

"The GPS is programmed. Just follow it." He paced the room.

"But why there?"

"Stop worrying. You'll understand soon enough."

"This whole little charade may have cost me my job, you know?"

"Your job is safe. If you still want it when all this is through." Craig dried his sweaty hands on his dress pants.

"Why wouldn't I want my job?"

"No reason. Just doesn't seem like it fits you." He tore off his tie and unbuttoned the top two buttons on his dress shirt. The heat in his room at the Element was unbearable. He'd switched down the thermostat, but it didn't seem to have any effect.

"It suits me fine. I help people. That's what I was born to do."

The hotel windows were opaque with condensation, but when he rubbed a spot bare, snow flurries fluttered past.

"Sure. I'll see you in a bit, okay?" He ended the call and tossed his cell on the desk. Why did speaking with her exhaust him? He wasn't trying to start a fight, but it seemed like her comments and questions were designed to make him say the wrong thing. Maybe it was all in his imagination. Sadie was in his head and not in a good way. He knew better than to let a woman under his skin. It would be good to finish this thing with Matt and move on to his next assignment. Several states away from her would be perfect.

JAVIER GROWLED DEEP IN his throat and kicked at the bits of glass on the kitchen floor in the girls' apartment.

They'd been here. The little dot on his phone pinpointed Sadie. The tiny brunette tornado who'd launched herself into her hero's arms, after he'd blown up his car, was nothing like her beautiful blonde roommate. That woman was high class with long legs and perfect pouty lips. She should've been a supermodel instead of a nurse.

The blonde was long gone; he'd noticed her absence after lunch. That was when he'd shifted his attention to her friend. A minuscule tracker slipped into her purse when she'd left it at the nurses' station was all it took to keep an eye on her, but she'd ditched her purse back here at her apartment before leaving. That little move was unexpected.

Javier dumped the contents of Sadie's purse onto the table and stuffed the tracker into his pocket. He had ways of finding them. They'd forced his hand, so he'd use whatever means was necessary to bring the doctor into compliance. It wouldn't take long.

Then he flipped the table over, ripped a lamp from the wall, and launched it into the glass partition that separated the living and dining areas. Served them right. He should torch the place, but nice guy that he was, he wouldn't. At least not yet.

Chapter Eight

Sadie slid into the passenger seat of the rental car and wrinkled her nose as the scent of vanilla and spice that clung to the interior hit her. She fastened her seatbelt using more force than necessary.

Brian's phone remained in her glove compartment, and a new phone awaited them in the cramped rental. If they had to rent a car, Homeland Security could've at least splurged on a mid-sized sedan. She was short compared to Madison, yet her knees touched the dash. Her brother wasn't a giant either, but at five foot ten, he barely fit into the compact car.

Brian nudged her shoulder. "It's okay. I know you hate it when your routine is disrupted, but this is the right thing, sis."

"How is that possible?" She frowned and rubbed her hand along the edge of the cloth seat. "It doesn't seem right. This has nothing to do with me. It's about my roommate's boyfriend. With Madison and Matt gone, this stalker guy has no reason to bother me. I'm a nobody."

"You're connected to both of them and to Craig, who's assigned to protect Matt. It's important to keep the proper perspective, so I'll agree with you that it might not make sense for the guy to go after you, but I understand why Craig doesn't want to risk it. He's afraid I'd kill him if something happened to you."

"No, he isn't. It wouldn't be his fault if some maniac came after me."

"If he knew there was a potential threat and didn't do everything in his power to protect you? I don't even want to think about what I'd do to him."

"Fine. I'll go along with this insane plan, but don't expect me to be happy about it." She folded her arms over her chest and stared straight forward as Brian pulled from the parking spot.

"Oh, Sadie. It's obvious you're not happy." She might've been happier if Craig had bothered to text her to reschedule their date. He'd known for twenty-four hours about this plan but hadn't prepared her. She'd been looking forward to it. How sad was that? She should've learned back in high school that the geeky girl did not wind up with the jock. That only happened in corny romance novels and chick flicks. A grown woman with some life experience under her belt should know better than to concoct some fairytale in her head about ending up with the guy she'd once pined over.

Ridiculous.

"The GPS is programmed for Philadelphia. Maybe you can see Mom and Dad while you're in the area."

"If Homeland approves, that'd be nice." And it would be. She hadn't seen her parents since Resurrection Sunday when her mother had requested her presence for Sunday service. Her mother had been in charge of special music, and it had been lovely. They would see each other for Christmas in a couple of weeks, but seeing them without all the extended family around first would be a blessing.

THE TRACKER JAVIER HAD placed on the chica's car brought him to a car rental place in Allentown. The brick building sat away from the street, but there were several people waiting at the counter inside, and a few more milled about outside. It was a bustling area with far more witnesses around than they'd had back in Danville. An unexpected setback.

The girl and her cop brother seemed a step ahead of him at every turn, but that wouldn't continue. He'd catch up with them. One way or another. Accessing the brother's contacts proved impossible, but a quick Google search on his own phone revealed everything he needed to know. The dad was chief of police in a town called Ridley. This was as good a time as any to pay their mom and pop a little visit.

And Matt's mom was coming along for the ride. He swiveled in his seat to meet the eyes of the handcuffed woman, a slow smile spreading across his face. "Don't worry. Your niño will do right by you. His affection for his madre is admirable. As soon as he realizes your life is in my hands, he'll give me what I want. Then, maybe I'll let you go." He chuckled. Then again, after this wild goose chase they sent him on, he might kill them all just for spite.

CRAIG HAMMERED AWAY AT the keys on his laptop. Homeland Security had booked adjoining rooms for Matt and Madison down the hall. Brian and Sadie were booked into rooms beside theirs. Homeland Security wasn't paying for them, but they couldn't keep him from protecting those he cared about. Thankfully, his government salary was generous enough for him to be able to afford the expense.

Quentin might be correct in assuming Sadie was no longer in danger now that they moved Matt, but it wasn't a risk Craig was comfortable taking.

His phone lit up with a call from the cell left for Brian in Allentown. "Hello?"

"Hi, Craig. It's Brian. We're in the parking structure. Do you have room numbers for us or should we go to reception?"

"Avoid reception. Head straight to the elevator and come up to the tenth floor. I'll meet you there with your keys."

"See you in a few." Brian disconnected.

Craig exhaled a shaky breath. Hopefully, Sadie wouldn't be too mad. He understood her desire to stay home and maintain her routine. Nobody liked it when their schedule was interrupted. At least he figured they didn't. It wasn't something he'd had the luxury of developing. Not since BUD/S, anyway. No one joined the Navy SEALs for a predictable life. These days a little predictability might be just what the doctor ordered, but taking a chance with a random girl was one thing. Dating his best friend's little sister was quite another. And she wasn't going to be happy about him not telling her ahead of time that they needed to postpone their night out.

When the elevator doors opened, he drank her in, completely ignoring Brian. A flash of appreciation flickered in her eyes, but hardness replaced it. He handed Brian his key. "Your room's down that hall. Left at the potted plant. Sadie's connects to yours."

"Where are you and Matt staying?"

"Just down the hall from you." Craig narrowed his eyes at his oblivious friend. "Give me a minute with your sister, please."

Brian shot him a menacing glare before stalking off toward his room.

"What do you want, Craig?"

"Walk with me? Get some coffee?"

"Aren't you supposed to be protecting Matt and his precious work?"

Four Homeland Security officers were rotating six-hour shifts at the lab, so they could eat, sleep, and handle other work-related responsibilities. Lisa Harper was on the job now. Fred Collins would relieve her, taking the overnight shift. Joel Bergen after that, and then Craig would step back in. He had twelve hours before he needed to return to the lab. "My relief showed up an hour ago. I've been waiting for you to arrive. I believe we had a hot date scheduled?" He wiggled his eyebrows.

"Could've fooled me. The date we scheduled was to take place in Danville."

He gave her his most charming smile and let his eyes speak the apology.

She huffed out a breath. "Fine. I need to get washed up first, but sure, I'll join you for a walk."

Craig couldn't stop grinning as he escorted her to her room. The girl next door was worming her way into his emotions. If he wasn't careful, she'd secure a foothold there.

Chapter Nine

Sadie showered and threw on a pair of jeans and a sweater. She'd stuffed a coat and a red scarf into her suitcase, so she wouldn't have to wear them in the car, but she'd known she would need them once they arrived at their destination. If she was going to be in the city at Christmas, she wanted to feel festive hence the red instead of one of her myriad other color choices. She knitted herself scarves. It was a hobby she could do while watching television. Her mom crocheted her scarves, so she had an abundance of them. One for every outfit, just about.

She knocked on the door that adjoined her brother's room.

He opened it and glanced sideways. "Going somewhere?"

"For a walk with Craig."

"Okaaay." He frowned. "Is something going on between you two?"

"You know we were set up on a blind date. He told you that much."

"Yeah. He thought it was funny."

"Well, he asked me for a second date. That was supposed to be after work today."

"Oh. That's what you were so upset about."

"No. I was upset because I should've been consulted before my life was turned upside down."

"Fair point."

"Anyway, we're just taking a walk."

"Do you like him like that? I mean I know you did back in high school, but that was never going to happen."

"Thanks for the vote of confidence, bro."

"I'm just saying. You didn't exactly have the same group of friends."

"Yes. I know. He was out of my league."

"Not at all. You're out of his. I love him like a brother, but I don't know if he deserves you."

A genuine smile formed. "Thanks. You don't know how much that means to me. I'll let you know when I get back."

Tears welled in her eyes at her brother's words, but she blinked them away and fled from the room. The sooner she caught up with Craig, the sooner she could find out if he truly thought there was a reason to worry.

DR. ALHAD SHARMA GAZED out over the Philadelphia skyline from his room at the Ritz-Carlton and gripped his phone, shouting, "What do you mean you're sitting outside of the girlfriend's roommate's parents' house? Why?"

"I've got to get a message to Dr. Wright. He left his cell phone in Danville. The roommate's mother is married to a cop, so he'll be able to get the message passed along. If he wants his wife to live."

"You can't be serious with all this? You should've killed the whole lot of them and detonated the lab before things became so convoluted. I have a hitman on retainer in case you mess this up and cost me millions. A mistake like that will not go unpunished."

"I hear you loud and clear."

"Good, get it done. Call me when you have what I need. Until then, pretend you lost my number."

Alhad stared at his cell after he disconnected the call. Javier had come highly recommended. Why? The man was sloppy. Too many loose ends. He enjoyed playing fast and loose and that didn't work for Alhad. No. He liked everything neat and tidy.

CRAIG PACED THE AREA in front of the elevator and studied the patterns in the tile. What was he doing starting something with Sadie? If it didn't work out, would they go back to being friends? Would Brian hate him? This was crazy. There was a reason he'd never allowed himself to see her in that light. Other guys at school talked about her looks, but he couldn't let himself think of her as anything more than his friend's sister. Not completely true. He'd considered it, but he'd tamped down the desire to date her, knowing that if he pursued her, he and Brian would have a falling out, no doubt about it.

He'd decked more than one guy himself who'd made comments about her curvaceous body. It was beyond inappropriate to think of her that way, no matter how true it might be.

If the Lord didn't give him strength, he'd never get through this walk. He should be straight with her. Tell her he liked her more than he should, but that a relationship between the two of them was out of the question. It would complicate things too much. He glanced up and his gaze slammed into hers. The fight went right out of him. She was adorable like a snow-bunny getting ready to go skiing before sitting by a fire in the lodge. Yeah. He had it bad. "Ready?"

"Can I ask you something? Do you think all this was necessary?"

He shook his head. "Just a precaution. Better safe than sorry, right?"

"Yeah." She smiled. "Thanks for that. My stress level dropped a notch."

Good for her. His blood pressure rose from being in the same vicinity as her. There was no way any of this was real. He couldn't possibly fall for her that fast. She smiled, and he reached for her hand. "Let's get going."

They strolled around, admiring the Christmas displays in various storefronts, and then they headed to Rittenhouse Square. The city was filled with the usual assortment of people from gang-bangers to businessmen and women to the party crowd starting their nights at the local establishments. He was pretty sure one gentleman standing by a streetlight was a flasher, so he steered Sadie as far from him as possible before taking a seat on one of the benches. "I wish we would be here longer. I saw a sign for the nutcracker ballet. I've always wanted to go."

"It might not be easy to get tickets this late," Craig said.

"Yeah. I know."

"But I'll see what I can do."

"There isn't time for all that," Sadie said.

"I know the circumstances are less than ideal, but I'm glad you're here with me right now."

Her smile warmed him. "Me too." His gaze fell to her lips, and the desire to kiss her overwhelmed him. A loud ring interrupted the thought.

"Harry? Wait. Back up. Tell me what happened." His eyes locked with Sadie's. "I'll be there as fast as I can drive. Call in the troops."

"That was your father. Your mother's been kidnapped. Her kidnapper is demanding to speak with Matt. When your dad got the call, he checked his doorbell cam. It wasn't a hoax. They have her."

Chapter Ten

Sadie insisted on joining Brian and Craig as they drove to the Ridley police station. Madison was sandwiched between her and Matt. They'd dragged him along, so he could talk to the kidnapper. It was the best chance they had for stalling until the cops could rescue her mother.

Craig's coworkers remained behind, guarding the lab.

The car rumbled along the pothole-strewn stretch of highway. A hint of new-car smell remained in the government vehicle, but it mingled with stale fast food and masculine spice. None of it was helping her uneasy stomach to settle. Her mother kidnapped. It couldn't be real. She squeezed her eyes shut and willed the dream to end, but when she reopened them, they were still flying down I-95.

Sadie dug her fingernails into her palms and blinked back tears. Scenarios of what her mom might be going through came in flashes. Shutting off the images proved impossible. Prayer wasn't coming easy either, but she kept trying. Whenever she started a prayer, the intrusive thoughts returned, but she fought them off and kept bringing her troubles to the Lord. He was faithful. It might not feel like it right now, but she needed him now more than ever.

Brian looked over his shoulder. "Hanging in there?"

"Best I can."

"Nothing is going to happen to Mom. She'll be home safe and sound before you know it."

"I can't figure out why anyone would do this. She's never harmed a soul in her life."

"I don't know about that. I have the paddle marks to prove it." He reached back and patted her knee. They both knew he had no such marks, but he was trying to lighten the situation, and as much as she appreciated his attempts, she'd prefer he acknowledge the gravity of the situation.

Craig parked beside a row of cop cars, and they all trudged inside. Her father was barking orders at Brian before they made it past the lobby. Then he saw her, and the look in his eyes softened. She hugged him fiercely and the tears broke free.

"We're going to get her back. I promise, sweetie. I'm going to bring my wife home before night's end."

She prayed he was as powerful as all that. But she knew not every family got the happy ending they hoped for. Sometimes bad people did awful things and they couldn't be stopped. Not without divine intervention, anyway. Prayer. That's what they needed. Prayer warriors and a lot of them. "Daddy, is there a phone and a computer I can use?"

He showed her to an office where she started making calls. First, she called her pastor's wife to get her mother added to the prayer chain and with an added promise from her to call other local churches and ask them to spread the word and get as many of the saints praying as possible. Then she called her mother's church and had them do the same. Then she logged into her Women of Prayer group on Facebook and asked for prayer there. Once she'd exhausted the possibilities, she bowed her own head and stormed the heavens with prayer, begging for her mother's life to be spared. If the Lord didn't grant her petition, it wouldn't be for lack of asking.

THE RHYTHMIC CLATTER OF typing and the hum of the forced air heat competed with the soft murmur of voices, emphasizing the tension in the Ridley police station. Craig stood against the wall with his arms crossed over his chest while Harry gave directives to his men. He'd called in half the force and most of the men who weren't called showed up anyway. Everyone in town knew the chief's wife was abducted, and they intended to bring her home. Mrs. Kline was as much of a mother to him as his own mom. He'd spent so many hours sitting in the warmth of her cozy kitchen, drinking milk and enjoying the delectable fudge brownies she'd made from a box. They were far better than ones his own mother made from scratch, but of course he'd never told his mom that. A lump lodged in Craig's throat as he pulled his focus back to the present.

Harry assigned an officer to check all the stoplight cameras and see if any caught the perp. Then he assigned several others to check with local businesses they knew had security cameras and ask to review them. They put out a message in the neighborhood Facebook group and got a spot on the local news. None of their actions took into account the reason Mrs. Kline was abducted. The thug who'd taken her wanted Matt's research. If Matt took the call due to come in less than five minutes, Craig would give the man whatever he wanted to save Mrs. Kline. And he knew Matt would do the same, but Homeland Security wouldn't authorize such a thing. They would want Matt kept away from this negotiation to prevent him from sharing his research. Craig had quoted the standard 'greater good' speech to Matt, but he knew his friend could see the doubt in his eyes.

"What do you want me to do, Craig?" Matt asked as they stood outside of the conference room.

"I want you to tell them whatever you need to so that they release Mrs. Kline." As the words escaped, his conscience was pricked. He couldn't save one at the expense of many. It wasn't right.

They surrounded a conference table where they were set up to trace it, but the chance of getting anything more than a ping on a nearby tower wasn't great. They'd have to hope something the kidnapper said or noise in the background would give away his position. Chances weren't great, but he hoped they'd get something.

A prayer or two wouldn't hurt. He thought of himself as a warrior. Someone who took battles head on, but this was different. To get through this case he needed divine intervention. Truth be told, he hadn't been great about keeping up with his prayer life. He bowed his head and squeezed his eyes shut, silently lifting a plea to the One who knew what he desired to say without him speaking a word.

The chief's line rang. Harry answered the call on the second ring. "He's right here. You can talk to him after you send proof of life."

Harry held his hand over the phone and spoke to the room. "He says to check my email." His secretary opened it and an image filled the screen. "That's not my wife," he said into the phone.

"It's my mother." Matt's face paled, and his eyes widened. He jumped to his feet, swearing. "He has my mom."

Craig pinched the bridge of his nose. This night kept getting worse and worse. What need would the perp have to keep Mrs. Kline alive if he had Matt's mother? They needed to stop this guy before things escalated any further.

He had a buddy in the FBI who worked as a hostage negotiator. A member of his former SEAL platoon. It was time to reach out. This situation was out of control.

CHAPTER ELEVEN

SADIE SILENTLY WATCHED THE emotions play out across Craig's face. She could tell the moment his jaw set and his eyes hardened that he'd come up with a plan and would take matters into his own hands regardless of the consequences. She couldn't let him lose his job trying to help her mother.

She studied the image frozen on the screen. Paneled walls. Pale gray floor nicked with age. An old podium, some rough-cut pieces of wood that had probably been assembled as a cross at one point, and a knee wall she thought might lead into a kitchen. It was probably white when it was painted, but had faded to a dull yellowish color. The clatter of covered dishes, the smell of casseroles and baked goods, and the hum of a microphone flitted through her memories. Familiar, beckoning. If she wasn't mistaken, Matt's mother was being held in the basement of a church in Drexel Hill. Or might be. She'd only been there a few times with a friend and classmate. The stage and the ancient paneling reminded her of the place, but it could be some other building with a similar structure. Nothing she could see on the screen was unique enough to only exist in that one location.

The church building had fascinated a younger Sadie. It had crawl spaces that splintered off in multiple directions, creating a maze of sorts. There was even a ballet studio on the first floor. She and her friend had played for hours in the crawl spaces and then sneaked away to dance in the studio. It was a good memory. If she shared her thoughts and they wasted time checking out the place, she would be responsible for delaying the real investigation and wasting resources on a possible dead end.

She might take a ride over there and have a look herself before telling anyone. If it turned out to be something, then she could call in the cavalry. It was risky to go alone, but wasting the department's time following a false lead would be worse. And she'd be safe enough as long as she didn't confront the kidnapper. Who was she kidding? Her memories were playing with her mind. The trip would prove she was mistaken—nothing more.

She didn't have her car, but she could call an Uber. Or ask Craig his thoughts. No. He would definitely insist on informing everyone. That couldn't happen. Not until she was sure she wasn't seeing similarities where there weren't any. She could be there and back in less than an hour. This was something she needed to do alone.

Craig wasn't surprised when Wally agreed to drop everything and come help. Most people could count themselves blessed if they had one friend they could count on in a crisis. Craig was blessed with thirteen of them. His twelve surviving former platoon brothers and Brian. It was hard to see through the turmoil sometimes and recognize his overflowing cup for what it was.

Fluorescent lights flickered overhead and the smell of burnt coffee mingled with pungent body odor, reminding him how long they'd been there. Harry's men needed time to rest and shower. The bullpen hummed with activity, papers were scattered across desks, several staff members talked loudly on their telephones. The tension was palpable.

He didn't see Sadie anywhere, so he checked the office she'd been using. Empty. Meandering outside, he spotted Matt and Madison huddled there in the alcove. Madison shivered in her light jacket, but it was obvious Matt didn't notice her discomfort. Craig removed his coat and handed it to Madison. "Have either of you seen Sadie?"

"Not since the call came in from the kidnapper." Madison's teeth chattered as she wrapped his coat around her shoulders.

"You should wait inside. Temperatures are supposed to drop into the teens tonight." A cloud of mist formed as he spoke, emphasizing the truth of his words.

Madison looked to Matt who gave a curt nod and held

the door for her to go back inside.

If Sadie had her cell phone, Craig would use it to track her, but he'd forced her to leave it in Danville. Where had she gotten off to? He went around the building and found Harry loading boxes of ammo and long guns into vehicles. The force of his actions and the set of his jaw gave off clear 'step off' vibes, but Craig ignored them and made eye contact with him. "Have a sec?"

"What do you need?"

"I made a call."

"And?"

"A friend of mine from the FBI agreed to come. Wally. He's a hostage negotiator."

"We aren't doing no negotiating. I'm planning to blow his fool head off."

"I get that, but he's coming. Wally will be here in case you need him."

"That's just dandy. The feds, yourself included, can sit around and watch the show."

"You know this is personal for me."

"But I don't want you to lose your job, so let Brian and I take care of it."

Craig shook his head. "Mrs. Kline's safety comes first. I have no intention of sitting around waiting for someone to cause her harm."

"Then join the party, sonny." He inclined his head toward the weaponry.

"I'm well-armed." It was true. He had one in his ankle holster, one on his hip, another at the small of his back, and two guns in his car. He'd known the case was dangerous before he'd come back home to Ridley. If he'd realized it would become this personal though, he might've brought some other weaponry along as well. This was turning out to be quite the adventure. "Harry, have you seen Sadie?"

"Not in a while, but I've been out here."

"It's strange. She seems to have disappeared."

"Maybe she hit the head."

"Yeah. I suppose that's possible." Something told him the ladies' room wasn't where he'd find her, but time was precious, and they had little of it, so he'd have to leave the mystery of where she'd disappeared to for later.

Chapter Twelve

Her Uber driver pulled up along the side of the church, and she slipped out. She immediately missed the warm, pine-scented air of its interior. The icy air burned her lungs and the wind howled as it slapped against her cheeks. She needed to figure out how to get inside.

She could try to enter by the door nearest the ballet studio. A lock on a door that old should be easy enough to pick. It wasn't a skill she possessed, having only watched a few videos about lock picking one night when she was bored, but it didn't seem that hard. That had been back in college, so it wasn't fresh on her mind, but she had to give it a try. She'd borrowed an old t-shirt from her father's office in case her first plan didn't work and she had to break a window.

She jogged up the pathway to the manse, but instead of knocking, she veered off along the hedgerow, the frozen grass crunching under her feet. Sadie crept through the shadows of the bushes along the concrete walk leading to the old stone church building. When she reached the door, she tested the handle. Locked. A few attempts at picking the lock with a bobby pin and a paper clip failed. Not a huge surprise. She moved along to a basement window, prepared to wrap the shirt around her hand for protection, but to her surprise and relief, the jalousie window was tilted out. Her hands, numb from the cold, cramped up as she slid the pieces of glass out one at a time and set them aside.

Climbing through, she scraped her side against the frame and lowered herself, holding on by her fingertips. Her grip on the sill grew tenuous. She estimated the desk beneath her seemed about six inches from the bottom of her feet. Drawing in one last steadying breath, she let herself drop. A loud clang rang through the air as her feet made contact with the old metal desk, and the impact sent a jolt through her body.

If anyone was nearby, they'd have heard her. After scrambling off the desk, she flew to the door and peered down the hall. When she didn't spot anyone, she hurried into the corridor, her footsteps echoing.

A cough had her ducking into an alcove. She wasn't alone.

Craig drove toward his childhood home, on familiar suburban streets lined with trees, their bare branches cut out around power lines. His parents met him at the door, and the familiar scent of his mother's pot roast greeted him.

"Have you heard anything?" his father asked.

His mother threw her arms around him in a warm hug before leaning back and searching his eyes. Her familiar rose-scented perfume brought comfort. "Is Eleanor going to be all right?" she asked.

Craig sighed. "I wish I had answers for you, but I don't. I'm here to see what evidence I can collect from the Kline's house. But I didn't think I should go next door without stopping here first and letting you know I'm here."

"We appreciate that, son." Dad scratched the back of his neck. "Want me to join you? Provide a lookout?"

"No, it's better you stay here. We don't want to get any more civilians involved."

"I'm going to keep an eye on things, whether you agree or not."

Craig released a laugh. "That doesn't surprise me." He kissed the top of his mother's head. "I hope to see you again before I have to head back to work, but if I don't get back here, know that I miss you both."

He crossed the lawn separating their house from the neighbors'. A churning in his stomach warned him something was wrong. It was Sadie, he was sure of it. She was in danger, and he didn't know why or how, but his instinct told him something was very wrong.

CHAPTER THIRTEEN

JAVIER THOUGHT HE HEARD a noise. Probably a squirrel or a raccoon, he'd seen evidence of both, but he couldn't take any chances. There was no way the cops would find this place. Not when they were expecting him to have kept the ladies close for an easy exchange. That's what they hoped for, of course, but that wasn't what they'd get. He stalked down the hall toward the noise.

No, he intended to have them leave the physical samples in a locker. A locker he would not be visiting personally. No. He'd send one of the women. He'd take up position with a sniper rifle. If they didn't return with the vials, he'd shoot them along with any officers sent to apprehend him at the pickup spot.

The cops always underestimated their opponents, so he expected bloodshed would be inevitable. All he needed to do was play his part.

As he made his way through the corridor, he caught a

whiff of something feminine. Shampoo? Perfume? The women he'd kidnapped hadn't been in this area of the building. He'd brought them in through the side door beside the breezeway that joined this part of the church to the sanctuary. He checked the first room. Looked empty. Then he saw it. The window was missing its slats. Could've happened before he'd brought the ladies here, but the scent on the air confirmed an intruder was present. A woman. And he'd find her and add her to his ever-growing collection. He opened the closet, slamming the door into the wall. She couldn't have gotten far.

SADIE HELD HER BREATH. She had made it up the stairs to the pastor's office. But the phone wasn't connected. It had been careless of her to come here without a telephone. What had she been thinking? Clearly, she hadn't been or she would've told her father about her suspicions or at least let Craig or Brian know. She was so afraid of being wrong, she hadn't given herself the benefit of the doubt. Now she would pay for her mistake. Unless she could come up with some way to salvage this situation. It wasn't far to the nearest door and if she went down the stairs by that door, she was fairly certain it would lead her to the area where her mom and Matt's mom were being held.

Should she try to rescue them or go for help? If she did the former, she could get captured or killed trying, but if she did the latter, he might move them now that he realized he'd been discovered. Then they might not find them again. It was an impossible choice. Drexel Hill was part of Upper Darby Township, and her father had no jurisdiction here, but she was certain if he called them, they'd cooperate and help him. She swallowed her fear and chose the hard thing, she would at least get eyes on her mom, so she could tell the cops what she'd seen. That should give them enough for a warrant if they needed one. And maybe it would qualify as exigent circumstances.

She made her decision and shot across the hall trying not to make noise, but the echoes in the building couldn't be stopped. Sadie reached the stairs, and ran down them. A breath escaped when she saw her mother and another woman huddled in a corner, both handcuffed to a chain that stretched across the floor. Her mother gasped when she saw her. "Get out of here, Sadie!"

Her mother's eyes moved away from her and locked on something behind her. Sadie looked to see what had caught her mother's attention. So much for playing the hero. The large man she'd dubbed "stalker dude" stood a mere ten feet behind her. The crawl spaces. If she could tuck into one, she could hide. He'd never find her in there. Then she'd wait him out. He was bound to leave eventually. She ran.

CRAIG WATCHED AS BRIAN pulled his patrol car into the driveway. He sauntered out to meet him. "Anything worth knowing on those tapes?"

"It caught a brief glimpse of the suspect making a left onto Swarthmore Ave from Morton Ave, but you can't make out his license plate. Best we could do was make and model."

"And?"

"Silver Toyota Camry." He pulled a folded printout from his pants pocket and handed it to Craig, who studied it a moment before handing it back.

"Looks like the same guy we saw hanging out outside of Sadie and Madison's apartment. Knowing the model of the car won't be much help. It's one of the most common vehicles on the road."

"Tell me about it."

"It's still better than nothing. What made the store owner think this was our guy?"

"You'll never believe this."

"What?"

"Take a look at this." He jabbed his finger on a smudge on the picture. "The guy said it looked like a face pressed against the glass."

"It looks like a smear of dirt to me."

"I know, right?" Brian shook his head. "Dumb luck, I guess."

"Or divine intervention."

"Yeah, maybe." Brian lifted a shoulder and dropped it again. "Find anything in the house?"

"Signs of a struggle. Potted plant knocked over, a

spilled cup of what looked to be herbal tea. There are at least a dozen prints on the glass coffee table, but one seems to have grease smeared in it, so that may turn out to be something."

Brian nodded. "Yeah. Dad was at work, so he couldn't have left it, and Mom cleans that table every morning when the heat's blowing because the dust from the forced air builds up so quickly."

"Then maybe we'll get a hit. I scanned it into the software on my phone, so I'm waiting to see what, if anything, it spits out."

"Now what?"

"We figure out what happened to your sister. I can't find her."

"Last I saw her, she was at the station."

"Same, but then she was gone. Something doesn't feel right about her sudden disappearing act."

"Hmm." Brian frowned. "I have a thought. Let's go check out the surveillance system at the station. See if someone picked her up."

"Why would anyone pick her up there?"

"They wouldn't unless she asked them to."

"Ah. You think she decided to do some investigating on her own."

"Don't put it past my sister. She's probably out there pretending she's Nancy Drew."

"No way. She's smarter than to check on a lead on her own."

"She's highly intelligent, but doesn't always show simple common sense that most of us take for granted. I don't think she would think twice about putting herself in danger."

"You were right to warn me off her. Falling for her isn't wise, is it?"

"Not at all." Brian laughed. "You've got it bad, don't you? Poor fool."

"Here I was thinking you were concerned for her."

"She can take care of herself when it comes to matters of the heart. She learned the hard way when she fell for you in high school."

"It was a schoolgirl crush. She didn't fall for me."

"I beg to differ, but let's not stand around jawing. We need to check that surveillance."

Chapter Fourteen

CRAIG PULLED A CHAIR up beside the computer tech and watched the surveillance tape play. Sadie had to have left on her own free will. There was no way she could've been abducted from the police station. Stranger things had happened. His stomach churned, and his muscles tensed as he watched.

Harry stood nearby, tugging at his shirt collar.

Craig glimpsed a driver pulling into the parking lot. Sadie slid into the backseat.

"Is that an Uber? Give me a close up of the decal on the driver's window." The guy manning the equipment zoomed in, and the chief cussed. "She didn't tell any of you where she was headed?"

"No," Brian said.

Harry tapped his fist on the desk. "Get on the phone with whoever you need to and find out who that driver is and where he took my daughter."

SADIE WAS OUT OF breath within seconds of taking off up the stairs, the big guy couldn't keep up, but he wasn't far behind. She ran through the corridor and then back down another set of steps, hoping he wouldn't think she'd returned to the basement. She stood silently, waiting to hear if he would follow, but his footsteps echoed farther and farther away. She'd lost him for now.

Doubling back, she found an entrance that would lead her into the crawl space. She wanted to save her mother and the other woman, but she couldn't do that if she was dead. Her best bet would be to make the kidnapper think she'd left the building. Then when she thought it was safe to come out, she could try again to rescue them.

The air inside the crawl space was thick with dust and what she could only guess was some kind of animal feces. Something she didn't remember from playing here as a child, but kids could be oblivious to the things that made adults squirm.

She found a wooden nativity blocking one of the passageways. It was the perfect place to hide. She moved Joseph and Mary enough to slide past them and then put them back where they'd been. If she was followed into here, the big man would think she'd gone another direction. He'd never guess that she'd taken the route of most resistance.

JAVIER STOOD IN A courtyard area between the old sanctuary and the main building. He'd somehow lost her. And she would give away his location, so he needed to move the women before the authorities showed up. But where would he move them? He hadn't thought that far ahead. For now, he needed to load them into his car and take off.

He trudged back to the basement and unlocked the chain from where he'd attached it to the base of an old radiator. Keeping the women handcuffed to the chain, he pressed them ahead of him up the stairs. "Gotta give the chica credit. Didn't expect anyone to figure out where you were. She's smart. Not wise enough to bring backup though."

The feistier of the two turned and pushed him. He laughed at her efforts. "Just for that, you and your friend here can ride in the trunk instead of the backseat. How's that sound?"

The woman spat in his face. He wiped it away, and forced himself to simmer down. Losing his cool wouldn't help the situation. He had moved the car onto the lawn as close to the breezeway doors as he could get it, then hit the button on his key fob to open the trunk. "Climb on in, ladies."

One woman complied, the other one shouted. A slap across her belligerent mouth put a stop to her shouts. He lifted her easily and tossed her on top of the other woman and then wound the chain around their legs to keep them from kicking to alert someone to their presence.

"Keep it up, and I'll kill her, and when I'm done with her, I'll find the chica and make her mine." He had a feeling fear for her daughter and the other woman's life might be the only thing that would keep her calm. Worth a shot anyway.

Chapter Fifteen

Craig stared straight ahead as he flew toward Drexel Hill with Matt in the passenger seat. It had taken an hour to get the location from her Uber driver. He said he dropped her off outside of an old church in Drexel Hill. The building sat empty, but something had drawn Sadie to it. They needed to get there, find her, and ask her what possessed her to go there in the first place.

Matt tapped his fingers on the console between them. "Why would Sadie run off like that? It makes no sense. Unless she'd figured out where our mothers are being held somehow. If that was the case, wouldn't she have told someone?"

Craig was pretty sure Matt's questions were rhetorical, and he didn't expect an answer, so he kept his mouth shut and swallowed hard at the thought of Sadie putting herself in danger.

He tried to work out her reasoning. The best he could

figure was she saw something in the picture of Matt's mother that made her think of this old church. The place wasn't even in their hometown, so it was strange to think that was possible, but what did he know. Whatever her reasons for going there, it was careless to go alone. But if she somehow believed that she might be chasing a false lead, she wouldn't have wanted to waste resources. Not the smartest choice, but it made a strange sort of sense. Quite possibly nonsense.

Sadie never had been a simple, predictable girl. Why would she be any easier to understand as an adult?

As they drew near, Craig slowed the vehicle. "I'm going to park on Mason. We can head over on foot. If, by some stretch of the imagination, the hostages are being held in that church, I don't want to put them at further risk by making our presence known by parking on Foss or Turner."

"Good plan. Any chance Brian and the police chief will think along the same lines?"

"You can count on it. They know what they're doing." He chuckled. "I can't say the same for the Upper Darby PD."

"I'd like my mother rescued rather than caught in the crossfire."

"We don't know that she's here."

"But you think she is, don't you?"

Craig didn't respond. He'd learned over the years not to make predictions. Sometimes his gut led him astray, but right now it was telling him Sadie was still here even if the hostages never were. And she could be in trouble.

THE CREEP HAD LEFT with her mom and Matt's mother. It was too quiet, they had to be gone. And it was her fault. If she'd told someone about her suspicions, they might've been able to save them. Tears streamed down her face as she pushed the nativity pieces out of her way and let herself out of the crawl spaces. A quick glance at the stage area told her that her suspicions were right. They were gone.

She sank to her knees near where her mother had been chained up like an animal and let out a strangled sob. A silent plea for help reached the heavens, and she trusted the Holy Spirit to make intersession for her since she didn't know how to put into words all the turmoil raging through her.

"Sadie?"

She turned to the sound of her name. Craig. He'd found her. Before she could respond, he was kneeling beside her and pulling her into his arms. "He took them. They were here, I saw them, but when he knew he'd been discovered he took them and left."

She melted into his embrace. He whispered comforting words against her hair and held her tight. It was a grace she didn't deserve. He should be hollering at her and telling her how stupid it had been for her to check out a lead on her own, but he wasn't yelling.

"It's not your fault. None of this is your fault." He kissed her forehead. "The Upper Darby Police should be here by now, and your dad and Brian are out there. Let's get you out to my car before they start questioning you."

He likely knew they wouldn't be nearly as understanding as he was being. "No. I'll talk to them. They need to know how I wound up here and why he left."

"They already know about the Uber, and from what I see here, I know it was the picture that drew you here, but how did you know about this place?"

"I came here once with a friend when I was a kid."

"And you remembered?"

"I couldn't be sure, but I thought it might be the same place. I wanted to check to be sure before I dragged everyone else into it."

"That was brave of you."

"And stupid."

He nodded but took her by the hand and stood beside her as she explained everything to her father and brother.

Chapter Sixteen

Craig and Fred both watched through the scopes of their rifles as Matt put his research and the samples in the locker. It wasn't his actual research. This was something he mocked up to make it look like the real thing at first glance. If Dr. Sharma inspected it, they'd be found out, but they'd made an educated guess that he wouldn't be the one emptying the contents of the locker. This bought them some time without giving away the formula for the antidote. If given more time, Craig had no doubt the shady doc would come up with it on his own, but he didn't think this whole exercise was so that he'd have it. This was about preventing the US from saving their citizens when the attack came.

Matt closed the locker and walked away. Forty-five minutes passed while Craig watched the clock tick at 30th Street Station. It wouldn't be difficult for someone to disappear into a crowd around here, so it was no wonder the perp chose this location for the drop. If it were him, he would've picked Suburban Station, but he expected the kidnapper wasn't quite as familiar with the area. So, how had he come across the church? The location was a choice one for his purposes. Just enough distance from neighboring houses to provide some privacy, but close enough that he hadn't had to drive far to get there, thus increasing his chances of getting caught. Where was he holding the women now? If he followed the same modus operandi, they might be able to figure out which abandoned buildings would fit his needs. That was what Brian and Harry were working on while the FBI and Homeland Security worked together to secure a stolen biological weapon.

Wally's voice came through his earpiece. "A woman is approaching the locker."

Craig's attention was drawn back to the lockers. He zoomed in on a lady a few feet from the locker they were watching. "It's Mrs. Kline. One of the kidnapped women."

Her eye was blackened and swollen shut, but she was alive. He needed to focus on that. He lifted a silent prayer of thanksgiving that Brian and Sadie weren't here to see their mother being used as a pawn in a deadly game. If they had been present, he wouldn't have been able to stop them from running out and trying to help their mom, an understandable response, but also a dangerous one. They didn't know where her abductor was, but if Craig were a betting man, he'd bet money the guy hadn't let her out of his gun's sight.

A rescue in a situation like this was far too risky. No. Their best bet would be to follow her. He'd placed a tracker on the package, another on the vial, and a third on the microchip. He shifted his sights to see if he could locate their perp.

Most likely, all of those would be found, but they had plain-clothed agents and officers assigned to several locations and ready to follow Mrs. Kline. If the trackers failed, he prayed they'd succeed.

JAVIER LET OUT A string of expletives. It looked like the woman was being followed. He'd made out the guy following her by his walk. He walked like a cop. They gave off a certain air. It was arrogance. They wanted to appear more confident than they felt, so they forced a fake pride into everything they did, and it showed in the way they sauntered along like they were the king of the world. This guy had it.

A push of a button set off an explosion in a trash can fifty feet from where the cop stood. If he didn't run to it, that would give him his answer. He was following her. The man looked that way but stayed on the woman. Clear enough signal that he didn't just happen to be here. Well, a little target practice never hurt anyone.

His index finger moved to the trigger, and he fired. A shot in the chest stopped the cop cold. He fell to his knees. The woman looked over her shoulder but kept moving. Smart lady. It wouldn't do for her to anger him.

"That a girl, come to Papa."

He met her in a tunnel and shuffled her onto a train with him, keeping her close with his gun aimed at her ribs. "You did good. I might even leave your chica alone if you continue to follow directions."

Her look of disgust was not lost on him, but he shrugged it off. He'd been dealing with hatred from her kind his whole rotten life. Now he would get what he had coming. Millions of dollars could definitely buy him a place on the beach in his home country if he so chose.

If not, he'd be able to send money home, even send for his relatives so they could join him. He'd never return here to this lousy country. The only good thing about it was that here he had found a way to make some money. Once he did that, he could live his life in peace. Forget about the likes of Alhad Sharma and find himself a little chica to settle down with. All his dreams would soon be fulfilled. He had that crazy franken-doctor to thank for it. Hard to believe that something good could come from the rotten little man, but he'd take the cash anyway he could get it. And Sharma was his ticket to freedom.

SADIE SAT AT A conference room table with her father and her brother as they tried to put themselves into the mind of the kidnapper and narrow down the possibilities of where the women could've been taken. If she'd told them about her suspicions, her mother would be home by now.

Her brother clapped her on the shoulder. "How are you holding up?"

She blew out a harsh breath. "I'm frustrated. This is my fault."

His eyes acknowledged her words, but he pulled her in for a hug and kissed the top of her head. "We'll get her back."

The tears she'd been keeping at bay for hours fell, and her brother patted her back, offering comfort she didn't feel she deserved.

Her father hit his hand on the table. "I might've found something."

Sadie and Brian both moved to stand behind him, so they could see his screen. He pointed to a real estate listing on a site that specialized in for-sale-by-owner properties.

"This page was the only one I could find in cyberspace with a listing for the church. The same website also has a listing for an abandoned art studio in Secane."

"It's worth looking into, but I'm not sure it fits his needs as well as the church did." Brian rubbed his forehead.

Dad nodded. "You're right. It doesn't offer as much privacy as the church, but it does have a rear entrance and since there are businesses on either side of it, and they're closed after hours, it would give him some freedom to come and go without being noticed."

"That would be a benefit for someone trying to hide two women." Brian grabbed his coffee cup and took a swallow.

"Shall we take a ride over there?" Sadie asked.

"You're staying here," Dad said. "Set a cot up in the office I had you in earlier. You should get some rest."

"I don't think that's possible."

"Try." He gave her a pointed look. "And for Heaven's sake, Sadie, don't leave the building while we're gone."

She lifted sad eyes to his. "I'll be here when you return."

Chapter Seventeen

Fred kept the crowds back, and Craig knelt beside Kevin who kept trying to sit up. Paramedics were on scene and had peeled away his shirt and found the bullet lodged in his vest. A close call for sure.

Kevin brushed away all the attention and reached out to Craig to help him rise. "He made me."

"I saw the moment he realized you were law enforcement. I tried to warn you, but it all happened in less than five seconds. The explosion then the shot." Craig held his hand out to get people to step away.

"We aren't giving this guy the credit he deserves. He's smart."

"He is. We're playing a deadly game of chess, and he's three moves ahead of us at any given time."

"Sounds about right." Kevin poked his finger through the hole in his coat. "Glad he didn't aim for my head."

"You and me both. You still need to have EMS take a

look at you," Craig said. "Then we'll have paperwork."

As much as he hated giving the man his dues, Kevin wasn't wrong. Their perp had drawn Matt out despite their efforts of getting him out of town and away from his usual means of communication. This kidnapper's genius was on a whole new level from what Craig had seen before. The guy didn't want to be ignored, so he made sure he wasn't. By kidnapping Matt's mother and then kidnapping Sadie's mom too, just to make sure Matt found out he had his mom, was a whole new level of wicked. He'd gotten what he wanted. Or, at least, he thought he did.

Craig felt like he was playing Russian roulette, except he was playing with the lives of others. Every move he made had the potential to harm Mrs. Kline or Mrs. Wright. When Sharma looked at the data, he'd know it was fake and all bets would be off. They needed to rescue the women before that happened.

Sadie told him about the events in the basement of the church, and it played on repeat in his mind. She'd barely made it out with her life and only because she knew more about the old church than the kidnapper did.

ALHAD SHARMA PULLED THE flash drive from the laptop and slammed it onto the desk. "A failure. That's what you are. Utterly useless. This formula is worthless. It's ciprofloxacin—a standard antibiotic that has no effect on viruses. They fooled you, but we will have that antidote or destroy it, one way or another." He clenched and unclenched his fists, making eye contact with Javier. "The auction happens in twenty-four hours. Fix this. Yesterday."

Javier glanced at the women. He'd planned to release them today, but a lesson would need to be learned. One woman would die, the other would live. Dr. Wright's mother's usefulness hadn't yet run out, so the other lady would have to die. Killing women and children didn't sit right with him. Never had. Not since he'd watched the cartel slaughter his madre. But for the kind of money Sharma was offering, he'd take out his own abuela.

"I'll get it done." He cracked his knuckles.

"I'm losing patience, Garcia. This is your last shot. Get it done, or I'll find someone who will."

"You threatening me, boss?"

"Take it however you like. Get the job done."

Javier waited until the boss left, then plopped into his seat at the table. He'd learned at an early age to take care of unpleasant tasks right away so he wouldn't have time to dwell on them, but bile rose in his throat as he thought about videoing the woman's murder and sending it to her family. He knew he had to do it, but it was inhumane. Committing this act would be admitting that he was no better than the monsters who'd slain his madre. Nap first. His head would be clearer after he took his rest.

SADIE CURLED UP ON her side on a cot. Her father and

Brian hadn't returned and they hadn't called. Neither had Craig. Her stomach churned, but she shut her eyes and prayed silently. After an hour of tossing and turning, she sat up and snatched the pay-as-you- go phone Brian had given her to use from beside her. Scrolling through the Google Play store, she found a Bible app that would allow her to listen to God's word. Once she downloaded it, she selected the Psalms and hit play.

King David had written most of them and his life was tumultuous, but he held onto his faith through everything even when his wives and children were kidnapped from Ziklag along with the rest of the women and children. The men with him talked of stoning him, but he relied on the Lord and with God's help they rescued all the women and children alive.

Eventually, the melodic words of the narrator lulled her to sleep.

Sometime later, her eyes flew open. She could hear voices. She sat up and tried to make sense of her surroundings. Right. The police station. A quick glance at her phone told her it was morning. Shift change. A cup of coffee would be welcome. After combing her hair with her fingers to make herself presentable, she went out into the bullpen area and her gaze slammed into Craig's. He met her halfway across the room with a cup of Wawa coffee. "Hope you still like dark roast."

"I do." How did he know that? She didn't remember him ever picking up coffee for her before. She took the offered cup and sipped slowly. "What happened last night?"

"You might want to take a seat."

"Did something happen?"

He ran a hand down his face. "The perp sent your mother to the pickup which wasn't entirely unexpected."

"You don't look happy, but if she'd been injured, you wouldn't be this calm."

"Your mom wasn't hurt. We had someone tail her, but they were made. Our agent was shot."

Her hand flew to her mouth. "Is he okay?" At Craig's nod, she drew in a sharp breath. "Where is Mom? Is she okay?"

"Honestly?" His shoulders slumped. "I have no idea. We had trackers on the data, but the perp found and destroyed them."

Sadie meandered into the office and took a seat on the cot. Her mother was out there with a maniac, and none of them had the power to get her back. If she'd been better, smarter, wiser, then maybe she could've prevented him from moving her.

Craig rapped his knuckles on the door frame, and when she looked up, his eyes locked with hers and he held out his arms. She went to him. How could she not?

His lips brushed her forehead, and she craved more. Needed the comfort he provided. She wrapped her arms around him, feeling the corded muscles in his back beneath the dress shirt he wore. He rested his forehead against hers.

Now wasn't the time to ask, but she needed to know. "When your case is over, are you leaving? Going to another part of the country?" She searched his eyes, noting the flecks of blue in their green depths.

Chapter Eighteen

"I don't know whether or not I'm staying in Pennsylvania." Craig stepped back and sank onto the cot.

Sadie lowered herself beside him and motioned to him and then herself. "So, whatever this is between us is temporary?"

"I'm not sure I know the answer to that. I need a few days to figure it out."

She dipped her head. "Okay." Tears pooled in her eyes, and he turned away from them, his gut churning.

"Are you close to the guy who was shot?" she asked.

It was just like Sadie to let him off the hook and change the subject. "No. Not really.

Kevin's going to be fine. Like I said, the vest took most of the impact from the bullet." He pinched the bridge of his nose. "This wasn't the first time I saw someone take a bullet."

"Your time overseas?"

"Not infrequently, but one face keeps running through my mind."

"Who do you see?"

"A brother from the SEALs. Someone I should've saved." He scrubbed a hand over his face. "Sadie, I'm not the boy you knew. I'm a man who has seen too much and given away parts of myself I can never get back." He lifted a lock of her hair and ran it through his fingers, reveling in the silken feel of the strands. "You deserve someone who can offer you everything you're giving them."

"What if I don't want anyone else?"

"Then maybe you should pray about it, because if we take this any further, we can't go back to what we've had our whole lives." He kissed her eyelids, and strolled from the room as if he hadn't just torn his own heart out with his bare hands.

Craig wasn't sure why he'd returned to the Ridley police station. There was nothing to be done there. His eyes lit on Sadie as she closed the office door behind her, eyes glistening. She was the reason he'd come. He couldn't stay away. She was hurting, and he wanted to be the one to comfort her. Instead, she'd offered him solace. And he'd pushed her away. Caused her more pain. Again. He was right about one thing. She deserved better.

Craig rose to his feet at the sound of Harry's voice booming through the station.

Sadie strode across the room to hug her father. "How'd it go?"

"No luck. We checked every property listed for sale within a ten-mile radius where we thought he could be holed up with the women. Even our most promising lead, an empty art studio in Secane was a dud." The chief took an unsteady step then stopped and gripped a desk for support.

"How long has it been since you last slept?" Craig asked.

Harry's eyes were glazed over. "Forty-eight hours, I think."

"You're going to collapse if you don't rest."

He looked past the older man to Brian. "And you?"

"Same. Maybe a little longer. Coordinating with neighboring cops and getting permission from owners to check properties made the night a long one. I'm ready to collapse."

"You two both need to head to the house and rest a while."

Harry crossed the hall and opened his office door. "I slept for a few hours yesterday. I'll rest again when Eleanor can rest with me."

Sadie narrowed her eyes. "You won't be any good to her in your current state."

"Fine. A couple of hours, then I'm back at it."

Hopefully, they'd find her by then. Lord, please. After Harry and Brian left, Sadie bumped her shoulder into his. "What about you? When did you last sleep?"

He frowned. "I'm not sure, but it's been a while."

"You should go rest on the cot back in the office where we talked earlier."

"Thanks. I may take you up on that. A twenty-minute power nap would be great about now."

"I'll keep looking at properties. He's holding her somewhere," Sadie said.

Craig only hoped Sadie's words were true, and Mrs. Kline was being held somewhere. It was far better than the alternative.

Inside the office, the scent of peaches lingered. He inhaled and considered going back out to find her. All he could think about was holding her again, but he'd pushed her away. It was the right thing to do. She didn't need to be mixed up with him, and he'd left the door open. If she decided he was enough, and she wanted him despite all his scars, he wouldn't turn her away. He wasn't strong enough to make himself walk away and break her heart a second time. Seeing her pain when he'd rejected her the first time had torn him to shreds, but he'd let her go, believing it was in her best interest. He'd known he was leaving Pennsylvania. Joining the military. He'd planned to make a career out of it, but on the day when Tony took a bullet to the head, multiple gunshots had ended Craig's career as a Navy SEAL. Somehow, when he shared the story, that part was always left out. It made him feel weak that he'd been ambushed. Dante and Wally had gotten him and Tony out of Dodge. Too late for Tony.

Homeland Security had recruited Craig from his hospital bed. At least the new job kept him from drowning in self-pity, but he'd accepted it without consulting his heavenly Father. And now he was pushing Sadie away without praying about it, all while hypocritically suggesting she pray. He rolled over on the cot and lifted his voice to the Lord. They had a lot to talk about.

SADIE STOOD JUST OUTSIDE the front door of the station. The brisk wind stung her cheeks, and she could hear the faint ringing of a bell. She couldn't see who was ringing it, but in her mind, she pictured a man dressed as Santa holding a red bucket. Shaking her head to clear the thought, she huffed, then turned to reenter the building, but as she did so she walked into something. Make that someone. Her eyes locked with Craig's.

"What are you doing out in the cold?"

"Aren't you supposed to be sleeping?" She frowned.

"I need to get back into the city. It's late, and we're having a task force meeting first thing in the morning."

"Oh." She looked down at her feet.

"You two are letting in the cold," the desk sergeant said.

Craig tugged Sadie inside with him and led the way to the room with the cot. "You could join me."

"Join you where?"

"Back at the hotel. In your own room, of course."

"You're confusing me." She rubbed her hand over her forehead. "One minute you're telling me to give you time, and the next you want me by your side."

"I don't trust anyone else with your wellbeing."

"You think you can go back to playing the part of overprotective big brother? I have one of those already. I don't need another. You were wrong. It's already too late for me to go back to pretending you're nothing more to me other than Brian's best friend."

He tugged on her hands, and pleaded with his eyes. "Please come."

"I hate you." She pulled her hands free.

"No, you don't."

"I want to."

He bobbed his head. "I'm sorry I hurt you, but I meant what I said."

"You said a lot of things. Which one did you mean?"

"All of them."

She rolled her eyes.

"All right. Specifically, I meant that I want you to pray about us. I don't want to ruin your life."

"You're being dramatic."

"And I also meant that I don't trust anyone, not even your father or Brian with your safety right now. You can't attend the task force meeting with me, but you can come back to Philadelphia. We didn't release the rooms we booked, so you can stay at Element just a few rooms down from mine while we search for your mother."

"I'll stay here at the house with my dad."

"Sadie, don't make me beg."

"Fine. You win." She tilted her head. "That was pretty close to begging, though. I'm counting it."

A slow smile spread across his face. "Okay. I begged."

"What will you do after your meeting tomorrow?"

He tugged on his ear. "Well, I doubt the perp is sticking to the suburbs. He probably moved after the church incident. The city is the easiest place to blend. And that's where the exchange was, so it's possible he's in the area somewhere. I'll search for him."

"What will I do while you're keeping busy searching for my mom?"

"Sleep in a real bed instead of a cot. Take a shower, you are getting a little ripe." His lips turned up in a teasing grin.

"Very funny. I smell just fine."

"Mmhmm. Like peaches." He flipped her hair behind her shoulder. "Seriously though, I'll feel better if I know you're close, and we can get together after my meeting to bounce ideas off one another."

Sadie grabbed a pen and a notepad off a nearby desk and jotted a note to her father. "Can't have Dad worrying about me again."

"Good thinking."

Chapter Nineteen

Craig dragged himself from the room the moment the meeting ended. He'd told Sadie he wouldn't be long, but two long hours had passed since then. After knocking softly on her door, he waited for an answer, but none came. Weird. She may have decided to take a shower or something. After slipping a note under her door to let her know he'd be in his room, he went to take a shower. If he didn't hear back from Sadie soon, he'd lie down until she called. Or until dinner. Whichever came first. A man could only go so long without a few hours of sleep.

When he reached his room, the king-sized bed beckoned him. He flopped down on it and closed his eyes. Next thing he knew a frantic knocking woke him. He rose and peered through the peephole then swung the door open to admit Sadie.

"Dad called the hotel, and they put him through to my room."

He inclined his head and waited for her to continue.

"Mom texted him."

"She got a hold of a phone?"

"She stole her abductor's cell phone and texted him. He said she sent a text and some pictures." She took a breath. "He's emailing them to you."

"Let's take a look." He flipped open his laptop and clicked into email. At the top of the list sat one from Chief Kline. "The buildings look familiar, but I can't place them." He tapped his fingers on the laptop, willing it to move faster.

"Do you think this will help us find her?" Sadie's voice had a strangled quality to it. He reached for her hand with his left and held on while he kept working.

"Probably a burner phone, so I doubt we'll get a GPS location from the EXIF data." He right clicked on the photos, hoping to find some kind of data, but it was blank.

She pulled away and started pacing. "Dad said he was going to use some kind of crowd-sourcing software to see if he got a hit."

"Let's see what we can learn through Google Lens then, your dad is probably already checking GeoFeedia."

"What's that?"

"It's an OSINT tool used to scour social media and other public sources."

"OSINT?"

"Sometimes I forget not everyone speaks law enforcement. Although with a chief of police for a father, I would expect you would."

"I haven't lived at home in a long time and new tools come out all the time."

"It stands for Open-Source Intelligence Tool."

"Got it."

"I'll check with Brian and see if they're having any success."

"Give them some time. I'm sure they'll call if they get a hit."

He opened the Google images search page, clicked the camera icon so he could upload the first of the photos. No usable results. After uploading the second image, he got something he could use. "Does this look the same as this picture of Spruce Street Harbor Park?"

"It's hard to tell from the angle, but it might be."

"Let's check the last of the photos."

Another hit for the Penn's Landing location. "Wherever he's keeping her, it has a view of the park, and the angle tells me she's on an upper floor. It isn't much, but it's more than we had a few minutes ago."

Sadie punched in a number on the hotel telephone. "We might have something." She relayed what they'd found to her father, listened for a moment, then disconnected the call.

"They got a hit on the surrounding buildings. Our location is spot on. He was able to narrow it down to the block, but not the building. Want to head out there?"

"Let me update the task force. Ten minutes, okay?"

She gave a brief tilt of her head, and he took both her hands in his and drew her closer. "I'm trusting you to stay put, okay?"

"I learned my lesson." The sadness in her eyes made the truth in her statement clear.

He dropped a kiss on her forehead. Couldn't keep himself from the displays of physical affection despite his resolve to back off and give her time to decide what she wanted. "I know my last meeting took much longer than expected, but I promise this time, I'll be quick." Even if he had to walk out on his team, he wasn't taking any chance of Sadie leaving without him.

SADIE WENT BACK TO her room. Her toothbrush was calling her. She'd collapsed the moment she'd stepped from the shower earlier and hadn't woken up until her father's telephone call, so she hadn't had the chance to freshen up.

Ring. She lifted the cell from the counter beside her. Brian. "Hey."

"The Philadelphia Police are insisting on taking over. Craig's not answering his phone. Is he with you?"

"He said he had to update some people on the new developments, but he should be back here shortly. I can have him call you."

"Do that." Brian sighed. "Thanks, sis."

Brushing her teeth and washing her face only took a few minutes, but by the time she was done, someone was knocking at her door. She swung it open expecting to see Craig, but her mother's abductor stood there grinning, gripping a pistol in his right hand.

"I planned to let you live. I did. You proved yourself a worthy opponent when you managed to elude me back at the church, but when your madre stole my phone, that ticked me off. My boss wants her dead. She's outlived her usefulness in his eyes. I should've killed her yesterday. If I had, I wouldn't be in this predicament." He forced his way into the room and gestured for her to have a seat.

"I don't want to move again, but she's left me no choice."

"What do you want from me?"

"Think you can get close enough to Dr. Wright to steal his real formula and the research that goes along with it?"

"It's locked up in a secure lab."

"Then all you'll need to do is convince him to give it to you. If you deliver it to me, your mother will live. A simple exchange. You have five hours. If the clock strikes midnight, I'll slit your mother's throat, and I'll videotape it for you."

Sadie sucked in a breath and counted to five. It was an impossible choice. He was asking her to betray a friend and quite possibly her country. From the little Madison had overheard of what Matt was working on, this could be a significant breakthrough she was being asked to steal. But it was her mother's life at stake. She had to save her mother first, then hope there was time to get the data back before it could be used for whatever nefarious purpose this monster and his boss had in mind.

"Your answer?"

"I'll get what you want."

"Give me your number. I'll text you a location for the trade."

"How do I know I can trust you?"

"You don't." A sinister smile touched his lips. "This is the chance you'll get. Take it if you want your madre to make it home alive."

Another knock on the door.

"That'll be your boyfriend. Make sure he doesn't know I'm here. I've got the room where your mother and her new friend are being kept wired to explode. If I don't make it back in twenty minutes, it's all set to go *boom*."

"I won't tell him you're here."

"Good girl."

Chapter Twenty

Craig waited for Sadie to open her door. She was taking her sweet time about it. When she finally pushed it open, he felt a strange shift in the atmosphere.

"Hey."

"Hey." He studied her. "You okay?"

"Yeah. Brian called my hotel room. The Philadelphia Police are giving him some trouble. He thought you might be able to intervene."

He pursed his lips. "Sure thing. Does he need me to call him back?"

"Yes. He asked that you call right away."

"You sure that's all?" He frowned. "Did something happen while I was gone?" Was it possible she'd thought about their talk and decided not to pursue more than friendship with him? It stung, but he should be glad. She was better off without his baggage.

"No. Nothing new. Just worried about my mom."

"Okay. Let's go get her then." He beelined toward the elevators. Time was of the essence. This maniac had already shown he wasn't afraid to shoot at police or set off explosives when he felt threatened. They had to make sure he didn't know they were coming.

"Are Matt and Madison joining us?"

"No. Why?"

"Matt's mom is in there, too. Wouldn't he want to be present if she's rescued?"

"I guess so. We don't bring civilians along on operations though. You're a strange exception to the rule."

"Because my dad is the chief of police?"

"No. We're not in Ridley anymore. It's because I care about you and your mother. This case is personal for me now that she's involved."

"You sure we should go there like this? What if we spook him?"

"Didn't you help me devise this plan fifteen minutes ago?"

"Yes, but I've been thinking about everything that could go awry."

"Leave it in God's hands, Sadie. We can't control all the things that can go wrong, but He can."

He returned Brian's call, then called his boss to ask him to handle the politics with the Philly cops. The drive over to the waterfront took about ten minutes, and he kept catching glimpses of Sadie biting her lip or chewing on her fingernails, a habit she'd given up when she was in middle school. She'd been a wreck since the moment she learned her mother was missing, but something changed when he'd gone to update the rest of his unit. He sensed there was more to her mood than she was sharing, but had no way of knowing what happened to make her fret. Or maybe there was a way. When they were done here, if they hadn't rescued Mrs. Kline, he'd try again to get Sadie to open up, but if she wouldn't, he'd look at the hotel call logs. There might be a clue there as to what upset her.

SADIE STOOD BESIDE HER brother.

"You need to stand back. This could get dangerous."

"I'm fine." She bit her lip and looked around. What if the guy decided to blow the place up with all the cops hanging around? They hadn't evacuated the building. Why hadn't they gotten everyone out. Weren't they aware of the threat? Of course, she hadn't told them what he'd said to her. How could she? Doing so would put her mother at greater risk. And there was Matt's mom to think about. This whole thing had blown up beyond what she could handle. If they didn't get a resolution soon, she'd wind up having some sort of breakdown. Her emotions were always close to the surface, but she was stretched taut like an electric line. And like a tree could bring down that live wire, a single action from the kidnapper could drop her.

Craig's words repeated themselves in her head. 'Leave it in God's hands.' How? She wanted to rely on the Lord, but she'd only been given two choices. Betray her mother or betray her country. Choosing was impossible. If Matt were here, she could ask him what he thought. He'd understand, and he'd want his mother protected, too. But he also knew what was at stake if she didn't follow the man's directives. He would understand the utter torment she was suffering through.

CRAIG GLANCED AT SADIE again. Whatever was bothering her hadn't let up. If this was about him, he wished she'd say whatever was on her mind. The distance between them might not be physical, but it was just as real.

They'd narrowed their search down to two apartments and they planned to breach them in a few minutes, but instead of looking relieved that they were close to rescuing her mom, Sadie looked more anxious than ever.

Leaving her behind, he rushed to where his boss Quentin Finnegan was hunched over a monitor.

Craig leaned in close so as not to be overheard. "Something's not right with Sadie. Any chance we can see her call logs?"

"Yeah. You think she's involved?"

"No. But something is off."

Quentin straightened his posture. "You mean like her mother being kidnapped? That'd put a damper on anyone's day."

"Of course, it would, but that's not it. Something changed in the past hour. If there isn't anything in the call logs, we should check the cameras at Element. I have a nagging feeling something happened back there. And she's not sharing."

"I can get Lisa into an interrogation room with her. If she's hiding something she'll get to the bottom of it."

"If you don't mind, can we try it my way first?"

His boss let out an aggravated sigh, but didn't argue. Ten minutes later, Finnegan gestured for Craig to join him again.

"You have some sort of superpower we should know about? Mind reading, perhaps?" Quentin asked.

Craig rolled his eyes and waited to hear what his boss had found.

Finnegan pointed at the screen. "This man was seen entering Sadie Kline's room less than five minutes before she left there with you."

"That's the same guy who was watching her and Madison back in Danville."

"Is it possible she's involved in this with him, and you're too close to her to see it?"

"No. Sadie would never have put me at risk and that guy blew up my car."

"It was Homeland Security's car that got blown up, and the head honchos aren't happy about it, which means neither am I."

"When we catch this guy, I'm sure they'll get over the financial loss. The tax payers are the ones footing the bill." Craig tapped a rhythm on his pants leg with his phone. "Sadie may not be his accomplice, but he could be coercing her into doing something by threatening her mom's life."

"Have a chat with your friend's little sister and find out what she knows before I'm forced to arrest her."

Craig nodded. If Quentin Finnegan thought she was in any way complicit with the kidnapper, he wouldn't hesitate to lock her up. He had to find out what happened in that hotel room before Sadie found herself in real trouble and did something she'd regret.

Chapter Twenty-One

Sadie felt a change in the air and turned to find Craig towering over her. "We need to talk."

She frowned. "About?"

"Come with me." He reached for her, and she took a step back.

"Where are we going?"

"If you don't come talk to me, my boss will put you in an interrogation room with my coworker. Would that be preferable?"

"I'll go with you, but can you please tell me where we're going."

"Our mobile command center. In that van."

"I'd rather we talked in your car."

"Fine. Let's go."

After he opened her door and she climbed in, he shut it with more force than necessary. He knew. She didn't know how he knew, but he did. And she didn't have an explanation that would satisfy him. She bit her lip until she drew blood. Not smart, but the pain distracted her from the chaos in her mind.

Craig slid in and slammed the door, staring out the windshield, not bothering to face her. A muscle in his jaw jumped. "Were you going to tell me that man came to your room?" He smacked the heel of his palm against the steering wheel. "He could've killed you!"

"The kidnapper said he wired the place where he has Mom, and if he didn't make it back in time she'd be blown to bits."

"Bomb squad is on their way. He blew up a trash can at 30th Street Station, but a trash can to an apartment building would be quite the escalation."

"I don't think he was talking about the whole building, just the one apartment."

"That would make the entire building unstable. He'd be putting hundreds of lives at stake."

Craig snatched his phone from his belt. "Finnegan, the perp made threats about a bomb."

"Gotcha. Anything else?"

"Still working on it. Wanted to keep you updated."

He cracked his knuckles. "What did he ask you to do?"

"What makes you think he asked me to do something?"

"Don't test my patience. I don't want to arrest you, Sadie, but if you force my hand, I will."

She swallowed the lump in her throat. "He wanted me to get Matt's research."

"How did he expect you to do that?"

"I don't know. But he wants it by midnight tonight or he's going to kill my mom and Matt's mom."

"Did he say why midnight?"

"No."

Tears flooded in, and she couldn't hold them back. Sobs that racked her body, and she rocked back and forth in her seat. Craig got out of the car. He was going to leave her. She didn't deserve his sympathy. The moment she walked out of that room, she should've told him everything, but instead she'd kept it all inside.

Then when he'd mentioned trusting God, she should've done so, but she couldn't bring herself to let go of control. The truth was she didn't have any control anyway. It was an illusion. The kidnapper probably planned to kill her mother no matter what she did.

Her door was wrenched open and Craig pulled her out of the vehicle and into his arms. He held her for a long moment before wiping her tears away.

"I need you to trust me, Sadie." His eyes searched hers. "If we're going to have any chance of beating these guys, I need you on my side, not theirs."

She sniffled. "I am on your side. I've always been on your side."

"Never do that to me again."

"How did you find out, anyway?"

"Hotel surveillance. You were acting weird, and you wouldn't tell me why, so I found out on my own."

"You spied on me." Her bottom lip popped out, but she couldn't be mad. Not really. She was relieved that he knew.

"And I'd do it again if it's the only way to protect you. Even from yourself."

"What do you mean? From myself?"

"If you'd followed his instructions, you could've spent the rest of your life in prison." He took a step back. "And I would've been involved in sending you away. Do you have any idea what that would've done to me?"

She picked at the cuticle on her thumb, avoiding his gaze.

"You put me in an untenable position." He lifted her chin, forcing her to look into his eyes. "If you were anyone else, I'd have you sitting in a cell right now."

"Then do it. Arrest me."

"No."

"Why not?"

His eyes shone with moisture. "I can't bring myself to take you in."

"If he finds out I talked to you, he's going to kill my mother and Matt's mom."

"I understand why you did what you did, but I don't agree with your choice, Sadie. And it isn't the first time you've chosen the risky path."

She sighed. "My mom deserves my loyalty."

"Yes, she does. But she wouldn't want you to go about showing it the way you did."

"What would you have done?" She searched his eyes for an answer.

"I don't know, but I hope I wouldn't have done what you did. I need to get back to the van. There is still work to do."

"Before you go, can I ask you something?"

He sighed. "Go ahead."

"Is it true that Matt's research has something to do with a biological weapon? That's what Madison said."

He raked his fingers through his hair. "I guess there is no sense in keeping the details from you at this point. Yes, Viper-X, a genetically engineered virus designed to be both highly contagious and deadly was stolen from a lab in New Mexico."

She gasped. "Wow."

"Matt and his team are working on an antidote for Viper-X. He thinks they may have it. It's currently in the final testing phase."

Sadie studied the ground, trying to wrap her head around the information overload. "Who developed the weaponized virus?"

"We did."

She raised her head and locked eyes with him. "We who?"

"The good old US of A. It was supposed to act as a deterrent to anyone who might consider using a biological weapon against us. Same idea as the Cold War with the nuclear weapons. If other countries know we have something that can decimate their population, they won't want to risk attacking our country."

"Sounds risky."

"It was. I'm sure we vetted the lead scientist developing the weapon, but he stole it. We don't know yet how he plans to use it, but we're hoping Matt will let us know it's ready within the next few days."

"That's a lot of pressure to be under while his mother is missing."

"It is." Craig shoved his hands in his pockets. "But Matt's project could save thousands of lives."

"And if he doesn't finish this testing phase?"

"We'll probably be forced to test it on anyone who contracts the virus." He shook his head. "I don't even want to consider what'll happen if we don't get our hands on the weapon or have Matt's antidote in time, but ... when you asked why he wouldn't be here, that's one of the reasons. One of our guys is with him at the lab. He's working, and he wouldn't have helped you even if it would've saved his own mother. He understands what's at stake."

"Does it make me a horrible person that I considered saving my mom over the alternative?"

"It makes you a human being. If I hadn't had time to think about it, I would've given the man what he wanted to bring your mom home." He pulled her around a corner, away from prying eyes. "God is our only hope here. If we think we're in control, we're only fooling ourselves."

"But what if He lets her die?"

"Then we mourn her death. But not without hope, since we know we'll see her again in eternity." He smoothed her hair down with his palm. "Your mother is like a second mother to me, but we have to trust God. His plan would never be for you to follow the instructions of her kidnapper. You know better. He'll use law enforcement or some other method to bring about justice. Whatever His plans, they don't involve having you breaking the law."

She dipped her head, recognizing how right his words were. "It's frustrating not being able to fix this, but God wouldn't want me taking matters into my own hands."

CRAIG SAT AT THE desk in their control center van, his knee bouncing as he studied the screen before him. He dialed Matt and waited as the phone rang five times and connected to voicemail. "Call me."

"Something's not right," he muttered. Next, he tried Fred, but no answer from him either.

His instincts had told him the perp was lying, but the bomb squad had gotten a camera in beneath the door. It was wired to blow if they breached the door. No heat signatures were found inside to indicate the presence of the two women. The whole message to Sadie may have been a ploy. The kidnapper could've sent those photos to Harry himself. Eleanor Kline may never have managed to get a hold of his cell phone in the first place.

This guy wanted to get his hands on Matt's research, and he'd found a way to draw Homeland Security and the FBI here to this apartment along with the Philadelphia Police. Only one of them had remained with the doctor. The lab was secure, but with this guy's propensity for using explosives, they couldn't be too careful.

They had to get back there.

"What's up?" Quentin Finnegan stood over Craig's

shoulder. "You thinking this was a setup?"

Craig jumped to his feet. "Yeah. We should get back to the lab."

"You go ahead. Take Bergen and Harper. I'll remain behind with the bomb squad."

Craig had his hand on the van's handle when Quentin cleared his throat. He glanced back. "Watch that you don't let that girl cloud your judgment."

"Yes, sir." He frowned. Was he letting her mess with his sense of responsibility and his duty to the country? He didn't think so, but she was affecting him.

Sadie had a sensitive heart and seeing it break was tearing him up. He felt an overwhelming desire to protect her. To hold her and never let go. And that was a problem. He'd thought they could go on a couple of dates, and get to know each other better. But the truth was they already knew each other, so the more time they spent together, the deeper he would fall, and he'd been trying to avoid falling in love with Sadie Kline since the day she entered the ninth grade back when she followed him and Brian around Ridley High. At the time, he'd promised Brian he would not date his sister. But now, they were adults, and Sadie could make her own choices without her brother's interference.

He'd even taken a part in the school play to be around her. Acting wasn't his thing, but she was. Within a few days, the girl with the lead had convinced him to take her out, and he'd been relieved because it got his mind off Sadie. Then he'd graduated and joined the military. They'd both moved on with their lives, but he'd never forgotten the sweet little girl next door. She'd grown into such an amazing woman. Not only was she easy on the eyes, she had a heart of gold, and courage to rival any Navy SEAL. Very few people would've gone into that church alone, but she'd taken the risk and made the rescue attempt. It was stupid, but it was incredibly brave.

Yeah. It wasn't his judgment that was clouded. His heart was the problem. And unless he was willing to accept a permanent position somewhere and stop traveling around the country for work, he couldn't let himself love her. She deserved stability and he couldn't give it to her.

He found Harry and Brian helping the bomb squad guys evacuate the building. After updating them, he searched for Lisa Harper and Joel Bergen to direct them back to the lab. They were standing around with some Philly cops eating soft pretzels and talking about the upcoming Eagles game.

"Hey. I can't reach Matt Wright, and I'm not getting an answer from Fred at the lab. We need to head over there." He didn't begrudge them the break, but they needed to get a move on. Keeping Matt's project safe was their top priority. Once his teammates were on the road, he searched for Sadie. Leaving her behind wasn't an option. She found him instead, popping out from behind the van as he passed it.

"Let's go. We have somewhere we need to be." He gestured toward his car.

She fell into step behind him and gnawed on her lip. It was red like she'd been at it for some time.

"You going to tell me where it is that we need to be?"

"Not a chance." He would keep the few details she didn't already know to himself. His loyalty needed to be to his country and to his job.

"I'm sorry about earlier," she said as he held the car door open for her.

"Let's try to put it behind us."

"You were right earlier. I should've been trusting God with this whole mess."

He may have been right, but he wasn't living what he was preaching. In his thoughts he'd been prioritizing country and job. Where was God in it all? His first priority needed to be the Lord. Everything else would fall into place neatly after Him, including Sadie. There was no reason the Lord couldn't protect everything and everyone that Craig loved. He didn't need to choose what mattered most. If he kept the Lord Jesus in His proper place, the rest would work out as it was meant to. Might not turn out to be the way Craig would choose, but he wasn't the one in control.

As they approached his car, a deafening crack split the air, and the ground around them shook. An explosion. He glanced up to see the windows blown out of the apartment where the bomb squad had been working. Sadie ran in that direction, but he reached her before she got far and grabbed her around the waist to stop her.

"Mom!"

Her tormented scream penetrated his temporary hearing loss from the explosion.

"They didn't find any heat signatures in there. She

wasn't there, love." Unless she'd already been dead. He thought it best not to voice that possibility.

Chapter Twenty-Two

Sadie couldn't move forward. Craig's arms were wrapped around her like a clamp. If he released her, she'd collapse, but he held on tight. Her father appeared in her line of sight. His eyes were vacant, his face void of expression.

"We don't think Eleanor was in there, Harry." Craig released her to clamp a hand on his shoulder. "Don't lose hope."

Brian approached, his chin trembling. He blinked away tears. "I think we got everyone out."

Craig pulled him into a hug and they embraced for several seconds.

"Now what?" she asked.

Her father and brother stared at her. The same question reflected back. Now what? How would they go on if Mom was gone?

"I need to get to the lab. I'll keep Sadie with me." He

lifted his eyes to her dad's. "I'm not supposed to tell you this, but we don't think Eleanor ever got access to the kidnapper's phone. It was a ploy to draw us away from the lab. Which means, she may never have been here in the first place."

Her father drew in a long, shaky breath. "How sure are you about that?"

"As certain as we can be without asking her ourselves." He looked down at Sadie. "This perp is clever, and he put a backup plan in place, but since we figured out what he was up to, that plan is no longer in play, so his only choice now is to steal the formula himself. I haven't been able to reach Matt, so my gut tells me he's doing that now."

"What about Madison?" Sadie asked.

"She's probably at the hotel. Why don't you give her a call?" He handed her his cell phone.

Sadie dialed her friend as they walked side by side to the car. Once they were inside, he pulled away from the curb and weaved around emergency vehicles. "No answer from Madison?"

"Maybe she has her ringer off. She could be resting."

That didn't sound right to him. With her boyfriend and her roommate both in crisis, it wouldn't make sense for her to turn off her sound. Nor did it make sense for her to let her phone go dead, but people could be careless. He shook his head. "Yeah. Maybe."

He entered the parking garage by the lab and Lisa pulled her car in beside his. Making use of the hand print and retinal scanner to gain access, he entered. Once inside, Craig stopped to take in his surroundings. Too tidy. Closed up for the day. Glancing at his watch, he frowned. "I knew something was off when I couldn't reach Matt. He never ends his day this early."

Joel bumped his fist on the counter. "This doesn't look good."

They pushed through into the back room and found Fred lying on the floor, his neck bent at an unnatural angle, unmoving. Craig felt for a pulse. "He's gone." He pressed a button on his cell.

"Quentin, I'm at the lab. Matt Wright is gone. We have a man down. Fred. We'll need a bus, but I assume you'll want it kept discreet?"

Sadie frowned and fiddled with a lock of hair that had come loose from her ponytail. "Other than the body, there are no signs of a struggle. Isn't that strange?"

Lisa took her time scanning the room. "With the security here, I don't even see how anyone managed to get past the front door."

"Unless Fred or Matt let them in, which would indicate it's someone they trust." Craig scratched his head. "Our missing persons list keeps getting longer."

CRAIG ESCORTED SADIE TO her room, and checked inside to make sure it was secure, then returned to the door. She stood in front of it, keeping him inside with her.

"Goodnight, Sadie." He paused. "Look, I know you've never seen a body outside of a funeral home before, if you need to talk about it..."

"No. That's not what's bothering me."

He lifted one eyebrow and waited.

"You're mad at me. I can feel the tension radiating from your body."

"I'm not thrilled that you kept the fact from me that a madman was inside this very room."

"Back at the apartment complex, I thought you'd forgiven me, but you haven't, have you?"

A muscle in his jaw twitched. "I forgive you, but that doesn't erase what happened. It's formed a barrier between us. You damaged the trust I had in you."

She trailed a finger along his jawline. "I don't like it when you're angry." His body reacted to her touch even as his mind fought to retain control.

"Disappointed—not angry."

"That's worse."

"I'll get over it, but this is the second time this week you kept something critical from me. Is that going to be how it is with us? You'll never feel secure enough with me to share what's going through that pretty little head of yours?"

"It won't happen again."

"Prove it." He lifted her chin and planted a kiss on her lips. It was chaste, but he hoped it was enough to show her his feelings for her hadn't waned. "Go to bed. I'll meet you here at seven. We'll have breakfast, and make a plan."

AT THE SOFT KNOCK, Sadie opened her room door.

"Ready?"

"Yep."

They rode the elevator in silence, but she still felt the distance between them.

"I said I was sorry."

"I know."

"Don't you believe me?"

"I'm not in the mood to discuss it. We need food. And we need to plan. Did you get any sleep?"

"A few hours."

"Better than none, I suppose."

"Hungry?"

She shrugged.

The elevator doors opened into the lobby, and Craig gestured toward the restaurant serving breakfast. "After you."

She picked at her scrambled eggs and bacon, but ate all the fruit that came with it.

"You should save your muffin for later in case you get hungry."

Not a bad idea. After wrapping it in a napkin, she stuffed it into her coat pocket.

Craig glanced at his phone screen then at her. "It's a text from your friend, Madison. I'm not sure what to make of it." He passed her his phone, so she could read the screen.

Madison: 39.89543361187762, -75.24695787340524

"Maybe it was an accident. A butt dial?" Sadie lifted a shoulder.

"Doubt it. The decimals and negative sign must have meaning. She's trying to tell me something."

"Does it look like GPS coordinates to you?" Sadie asked.

"Let's enter them and see what we come up with." He plugged the numbers into an app. "It's the John Heinz National Wildlife Refuge."

"I know it. It's in Tinicum. Back when I foolishly believed that I could save the earth, I went to a few environmental summits there."

"How were they?"

"Just a bunch of politicians and activists spending their days droning on about all the good they planned to do, but never accomplishing anything worthwhile. Tried to get some people interested in cleaning streams or picking up litter, but it was more about politics. And often their politics didn't align with my values, so I stopped participating."

His hand moved to her face and his thumb caressed her jaw. "Sounds like you made the right choice. Never pays to do something that doesn't align with your morals."

She swallowed hard, and her eyes searched his. Could she lean on this man? Trust him with her heart? Past experience said no, but she wanted the answer to be yes.

He leaned close and took her hands in his. "This could be a trap. Why doesn't Madison call me? How can we be sure those texts are coming from her?" He refrained from mentioning Homeland Security believed her mother hadn't sent any texts either, that they thought it had all been a ruse. If he opened up about what he knew, she'd be upset that he hadn't said anything sooner, and she'd wonder once again if her mother was alive or dead. There wasn't time for grief right now. He could share all this later. Hopefully, they'd find her mom first, making the whole pending conversation moot.

"What if she can't call? Madison might've found a way to keep it on her person."

"These criminals are too sophisticated to make stupid mistakes like missing a cell phone."

"Anything's possible, right?" she asked.

"Want to take a drive over there with me, or should I drop you at the hotel?" Craig scratched the stubble on his chin.

"Last time you left me alone there I was threatened at gunpoint." The image her words evoked left his stomach roiling.

"Good point. I'm not leaving you anywhere. Just give me a second to call my team and then we'll hit the road."

Chapter Twenty-Three

They pulled into the parking lot, and Craig hopped from the vehicle. The moment they'd left the lab, he'd called Quentin Finnegan to update him on what they'd found. He'd fumed about how his incompetent subordinates lost track of Matt Wright. He wasn't wrong, but since Craig had been with his boss when it happened, he didn't think he was the person on whom he should be venting his frustration. Nevertheless, he listened patiently as they drove toward Tinicum.

The wildlife refuge always felt like a study in contrasts to him. It wasn't far enough removed from Philadelphia to get away from the pollution. The air held a hint of scent that wasn't from the marsh lands and the hum of the city wasn't completely eradicated. It felt like he hovered on the edge of two worlds. As he opened Sadie's door, his phone buzzed.

"It's another text from Maddie. Or the kidnapper." Craig handed Sadie his phone. The bright sun reflected off the snow-covered ground. She squinted at the screen.

Madison: Wetland Loop Trail. Bird Blind.

"That's not close. The walk in will make us easy targets," he said.

She sighed, but said nothing.

Lisa and Joel drove up and joined them beside Craig's car.

"So, what do we do, ignore her?" Sadie asked.

"We're here, so obviously we're not planning to leave her in harm's way."

"If we can't go get her, what are we going to do?

"We'll do the unexpected. Handle things with a bit of finesse." He popped the trunk. Joel lifted the unmanned aerial vehicle from the box keeping it from bouncing around.

"A drone?"

"UAV surveillance should give us an idea of what's waiting for us near that bird blind."

"Do you always have a drone around with you?"

"Most of the time. It's come in handy more than a few times."

"Did you have one in your vehicle when it exploded?"

He clasped the back of his neck. "Yes. A top-of-the-line model. I don't think my bosses are too thrilled about it."

"I'm sure it cost less than the SUV they lost."

That was little consolation.

JAVIER TAPPED THE CELL phone against his leg. What was taking the boss so long? He'd bashed the girl over the head with a rock after their hike, but now she was starting to moan. Soon she'd be fully awake, and he'd have to deal with her before she started screaming. He was hoping he'd have time to make the exchange and leave her in the blind before anyone else showed up. Maybe someone would find her. Maybe they wouldn't. But she wouldn't be his problem any longer.

He glanced at his phone screen. Sharma was supposed to meet him there twenty minutes ago. It was a desolate place on the twenty-second of December. He imagined most people were finishing up their Christmas shopping. There were a few brave people out hiking in the elements, so witnesses could arrive at any time. He didn't like the thought of killing. There were other ways to take care of problems, but Sharma had been rather detailed about how he wanted things handled and none of his usual methods were acceptable to the boss. His gaze flicked to Dr. Wright's prone figure a few feet away. Some deaths couldn't be avoided.

The good doctor had chosen his own downfall when he'd tried to pass off false data for the real thing. His death would be on his own conscience. Did dead people have a conscience? A morbid question Javier couldn't answer. Instead, he turned his thoughts to more pleasant things. Soon he'd be sipping frozen Margaritas on a sun-drenched beach without a care in the world. He wouldn't even complain about the little pink umbrellas as long as he could dig his toes into the warm sand and relish the rays on his bare skin. The good life. Closing his eyes, he could taste the salt in the air.

SADIE SAT ON A bench with Lisa Harper and they both watched as Craig operated the drone. The device sent a live video feed to Craig's phone, allowing him to monitor its progress.

"Whoa." He hit something that let him zoom in on the feed and they all stared at his small screen.

"Is that Dr. Wright?" Lisa asked.

Craig's brow furrowed. "I think it's him. Doesn't look good. Let's get some backup here."

The sight of Matt lying motionless in the muddy snow at the edge of the water left her cold inside. First her mother's abduction, then the explosion, and now this. She felt her control slipping. If Matt was alive, he wasn't conscious. Prayers welled up from somewhere deep inside, and she slipped down to the ground, not caring about the snow seeping into her jeans and soaking them. "Lord, please spare them," she whispered.

Within minutes, the first of the sirens sounded, followed by the flash of red and blue lights and the screech of tires.

Craig held out a hand and she accepted his offer of assistance, rising to her feet. "I'm going to head out there, but I'm not going to be able to do my job if you're there with me. I'll be concentrating on you instead of getting this guy."

Sadie clutched the cross that rested in the hollow of her throat. "I'll wait here."

Craig grabbed a blanket from the trunk and handed it to her. "This should keep you warm while I'm out there." He bent down and placed a kiss on her forehead, but it wasn't enough.

She reached up and planted her lips against his to reassure herself that their connection was real. And that they were going to get through this somehow. "Come back to me."

"I'm sorry, Sadie. I shouldn't have dragged you out here. You should be back at the hotel."

"I made the decision not to go back. You know that."

Something she couldn't identify lit his eyes, but it was gone in an instant. Had she imagined it? He placed a hand on the small of her back, leading her to the car. She climbed into the passenger seat and covered herself, holding the blanket to her nose so she could smell Craig on it. She watched through the windshield as he climbed onto the back of an ATV. Within minutes, he was out of sight and Craig's boss and a Tinicum cop remained in the parking lot.

Chapter Twenty-Four

THEY PARKED THE ATV along the side of the trail and hiked toward the bird blind. It wasn't ideal since they wanted to get to Matt as fast as possible, but they didn't want to risk provoking a shootout. The plan was for them to come from one side, while another team approached from a different direction. They would cut him off, so the only way out was across the water. It wasn't frozen enough for a clean getaway. If he tried to cross the ice, he'd fall through sooner or later. It wasn't the ending they wanted, but it was preferable to him wreaking havoc on the country with his stolen weapon.

A gunshot split the silence. "Get down." They both dropped to the ground. He radioed to the other group to get their position. After determining they were out of harm's way, he gestured to a tree. "Head there. I'll cover you." He laid down fire while Lisa dove behind a tree. More gunfire peppered the ground all around him. Lisa gestured for him to get to safety, then lifted her rifle and opened fire.

He ran for cover, weaving so he wouldn't be an easy target to hit.

A deafening noise sounded, and he shuddered to think of what their suspect might've blown up this time. The trash can at 30th Street Station was relatively harmless, but the explosion at the apartments could've taken out hundreds. He hoped the bomb wasn't rigged with Viper-X. If it was, anyone within a five-mile radius would die and if those infected weren't contained fast enough, it could spread to thousands more.

The man they'd been tracking was reckless, but not suicidal. Gunfire ceased, probably reloading.

Smoke rose in the distance. The parking lot. A car bomb? *Please, let Sadie be safe.*

"Let's move in," he shouted. They dodged from tree to tree, moving toward the blind. He scrambled to get closer to Lisa and motioned to her. "I spotted him. It looks like he's the only shooter."

"Hostages?"

"I don't see them, but we know Matt's out there."

She studied the area through the scope of her rifle. "Dead most likely."

"We'll find out when we get there."

Another volley of shots came their way, and they remained covered until he had to reload again.

Joel radioed. "I have joy."

Craig hated life-and-death calls, but too many lives were in danger to risk letting the chance go. "Take the shot."

"He's down."

They moved in cautiously. Lisa kicked the AR out of the suspect's reach.

Craig glanced at the man's lifeless eyes. The accomplice. Someone moaned, and he turned toward the sound, leading with his weapon. Madison lay prone beneath the wooden structure. Only her feet poked through. He rushed to her side and scanned her for injuries. Her eyes popped open.

"Are you hurt?"

She winced. "My head."

He inspected the injury to the back of her head then removed his backpack for his first-aid supplies. "Take care of her." He passed his kit to Lisa and went to where he knew he would find Matt. His pale skin had a grayish pallor to it. He closed his eyes against the pain, but a groan drew his gaze back to Matt's face. Craig placed his fingers to Matt's neck and detected a thready pulse. He exhaled, lifting a praise to the Lord.

DISTANT GUNFIRE ECHOED THROUGH the wildlife refuge, and Sadie struggled to stay in her seat. Then an explosion cracked the air, and Sadie's heart jumped to her throat. This was what happened at the apartment. Her mother's kidnapper was here. Did he hurt Craig? Her mom?

She leapt from the vehicle to ask Craig's supervisor

what he knew. She found him reclining against a police car.

She waved a hand in front of her face to disperse some of the black smoke. "What's happening?"

"Car bomb."

"Was anyone hurt?"

"Agents and officers have it under control. No need to worry."

"Was Craig injured?"

"Ma'am, this is a Homeland Security operation. It'd be best if you stayed inside the car."

She returned to Craig's vehicle and slammed the door shut. Reminding herself that agents and officers were trained to stay cool under pressure, so his lack of emotion didn't mean anything.

Digging her nails into her hand, she let the tears fall. Sitting here wasn't accomplishing anything. She needed to know what was happening beyond her field of vision for her own sanity.

Ten minutes ticked by and all she could hear was the sound of her own breathing and the occasional radio transmission that she couldn't decipher. Activity on the trail drew her notice, and she slipped from the car again, not caring what the Field Operations supervisor had to say about it. She didn't work for him. Jogging to the trail, she noticed the stretcher carried by two paramedics. Matt didn't look good. She scanned the crowd of first responders until her gaze locked on Craig's. He was all right. A second stretcher arrived carrying Madison. Sadie rushed to her friend's side.

"Are you okay?"

"I'm alive."

"What happened?"

"I went to the lab to meet Matt for lunch and when he came out into the lot to meet me, we were ambushed."

The implications of that dug under her skin. "Did they get their hands on his work?"

Her friend shrugged. "I don't know what they got."

Didn't they have enough to force his hand when they were holding his mom? Why take his girlfriend, too? These men needed to be stopped before anyone else got hurt.

"Ma'am, we need to get you into the ambulance," an EMT said.

Sadie squeezed Madison's hand and took a step back.

Craig's boss Quentin inserted himself between her and Craig. "I'll go to the hospital to get the girl's statement. You handle the scene here. Then get the paperwork filed on the shooting."

"Will do, boss." Craig stood back and watched as they loaded Madison and Matt into ambulances and rode off.

After they were gone, Craig draped an arm around her shoulder. "She'll be okay."

"What about Matt?"

He shook his head. "He's in God's hands."

"What happened out there?"

"We took out their kidnapper, but we didn't secure Viper-X or the antidote. They're both out there somewhere."

"Was it the guy who took my mom?"

"Yes."

"You can't question him if he's dead! How are we going to find her?" She heard the accusation in her voice, but with her stomach roiling and her head pounding, the last thing she felt like concerning herself with was keeping her tone pleasant.

"We didn't have much choice. He was shooting at law enforcement, and he had two hostages on site."

Silent tears streamed hot trails down her frozen cheeks. "I need to be with my father and brother."

"I have some paperwork I need to do, but I can take you back to your parents' house first."

ALHAD USHERED HIS BROTHER into his room at the Ritz-Carlton, noting the case he was toting with him. He smiled and let out a relieved breath. "You have it. Good."

"That maniac you hired wired his vehicle to explode. I had to disarm it before I could get your precious work back."

"Is he dead?"

"What do you think?"

"He shouldn't have tried to steal what was mine. I might've let him live if he hadn't."

Rajesh laughed. "You never had any intention of keeping him alive. Did you forget who you're talking to?"

Alhad made a swatting motion in the air. "You're right, of course."

"I know." Rajesh grinned.

"Any luck getting the antidote?"

He held up a flash drive and a vial. "Wasn't easy. Had to use my authority to coerce it from Matt's girlfriend. Javier used her to get inside the lab, but Wright was smarter than your thug. He used his girl as a mule. I don't think she quite understood what she had shoved in the pocket of her coat."

"Did you take care of her?"

"Too many people around." He walked to the window overlooking the city view. "She handed her boyfriend's project over to a Field Operations supervisor with Homeland Security and was happy to be rid of it. The girl won't be a problem."

"If this is all she had, they likely have more antidote at the lab."

"I don't think so. Those were destroyed by my inside man."

"And where is he?"

"Your man broke his neck."

"Dead?"

Rajesh nodded.

CHAPTER TWENTY-FIVE

CRAIG PULLED INTO THE Klines' driveway and gripped the wheel, staring straight ahead, his jaw clenched. They should've found Mrs. Kline and Mrs. Wright by now. With the perp out of the picture, they had little to go on to find them. The realization that it was most likely a recovery operation and not a rescue brought bile into his throat. A gentle touch on his shoulder pulled him from his thoughts. He covered Sadie's hand with his own.

"None of this is your fault, Craig."

"It sure feels like it is." He cradled her face, and his thumb brushed her cheek. She was so beautiful. It wasn't a newsflash really. He'd always recognized her attractiveness, but something inside him had changed, and he saw her differently than before. Her inner beauty made her even more desirable, but now wasn't the time to dwell on it. "Let's head inside before your father comes out here with his rifle."

A hint of a smile warmed her face. They walked to the door together, and he drew her hands into his own, rubbing the backs with his thumbs. "I'm not giving up on your mom."

"Neither am I." She stood on her tiptoes and brushed her lips across his.

He released her hands and tugged her close, crushing her to his chest, deepening her kiss. When he pulled back, he gazed into her eyes. "How can I feel so close to you when we were apart for so long?"

"I don't know, but the feeling is mutual. When you were on that trail at Heinz, and I heard that gunfire ... well, suffice it to say, I was afraid I'd lost you."

The door swung open, and her father stood there, his gaze shifting between the two of them. "I'm not going to ask."

Craig didn't release her. He inhaled the scent of peaches and placed a final kiss on the top of her head before stepping away to try to collect his muddled thoughts.

"Harry, the man who kidnapped your wife was taken out this evening. I need to head to our Philadelphia office and fill out some paperwork. I'm going to have to sleep for a few hours, but I won't give up until we find Mrs. Kline." They had to find Mrs. Wright, too.

Homeland Security's concern was for securing Viper-X. The missing women weren't even on their radar, but Craig wouldn't stop looking. Even if it got him fired.

Harry clasped his hand. "Thanks, son. I know you're

doing everything in your power." He turned his gaze to his daughter, and she stepped closer to hug her dad.

After one last look at Sadie, Craig left.

CHRISTMAS EVE. SEEMED SOMEHOW appropriate to him that this so-called Christian nation should be sold out on a day when they celebrated their so-called savior. Nobody was going to save them this time. A twinge of unease pricked against his spine, but he dismissed it.

He didn't hate his adopted country, and he was fond of the family who'd taken him in. They'd been good to him. Had given him a fine life and a good education, but something was missing. He had always wanted more. He'd wanted to fit in. That hadn't been a possibility in his neighborhood. With those people. This was his chance.

"Let the games begin." With a tap of his mouse, Alhad Sharma opened the auction. He now had his briefcase back with the Viper-X samples resting securely inside, along with Wright's antidote and its accompanying research.

The bids poured in, and his discomfort over selling out his adopted country dissipated as the number of zeros that would soon be in his bank account increased.

IT WAS CHRISTMAS EVE. Craig felt the excitement in the hotel lobby with its giant tree decorated with pale blue and peach ornaments and ribbons. It was beautiful, but it wasn't homey. What he longed for was a Fraser fir decorated with childish handmade ornaments and packages strewn haphazardly beneath it. He wanted a whole brood of kids to fill his life with. Living in temporary rental homes wasn't living at all. Family mattered, and he wanted one of his own.

After one last glance at the tree and the guests, he strode to reception to check out. As he did, he lifted a prayer asking for help finding the women. When he reached the counter, he paused. The man had been in Sadie's room. They'd never checked the footage to see what time he'd arrived. What if he'd been there all along keeping an eye on the investigation from inside the same place the agents were staying. Craig made a call and asked to speak to a manager.

A man approached him a few minutes later, holding out his hand. "Geoffrey Stapleton." He smiled. "How can I help you today?"

Craig flipped open his credentials. "Craig Malone with Homeland Security. We served Element by Westin with a warrant yesterday to review footage from your tenth floor. A man entered a woman's room unlawfully on that floor. That same man was killed in a standoff last night, so we're going to need to review the rest of your footage to find out if he was a guest."

"Certainly, I can help you with that. Follow me."

The manager took him to a security room filled with monitors where another man sat. "Jerome. This gentleman is law enforcement. Please give him whatever he needs."

It was a small miracle that the man didn't ask for another warrant or for him to produce the first one. While it wouldn't have been too much of a hassle to do so, it would've taken valuable time that would be better spent reviewing the footage. He was impressed with the setup the security office had. Jerome brought up the footage outside of Sadie's room. Taking a still from the video, he ran the man's face through their system and got several hits. The man had arrived shortly after Brian and Sadie. Despite all the precautions they'd taken, he'd somehow figured out where Sadie was. At that point, he hadn't known where the secondary lab was. If he had, he wouldn't have needed Matt's mother. And he'd taken Sadie's mother instead of Sadie because she was with him. Easier to target her mother to get Matt's attention than it was to kidnap Sadie right under the noses of several federal agents and a cop. Bringing Sadie to Philadelphia might've kept her safe, but it may have cost her mother her life. Craig pushed the thought away. They didn't yet know that Mrs. Kline was dead, and until they did, they needed to operate as if she and Mrs. Wright were both alive.

"I'M SORRY, BUT HE stepped away from his desk," Quentin's secretary stated.

Craig couldn't believe he'd gone back to Washington DC while they were in the midst of the biggest case of his career. "Can you go find him?"

"I'll look for him." Craig tapped his foot impatiently while waiting for his boss to come on the line.

"Quentin Finnegan speaking."

"It's Craig."

"What do you have?" Quentin asked.

"I think we tracked where the virus was yesterday, but it's gone now. The perp Joel shot yesterday placed a metal briefcase in the trunk of his car before leaving his hotel. The same one that detonated at Heinz. No sign of it now. His accomplice must have removed it before setting off the explosion."

"Hmmm."

"Are you going to return to Philly?" Craig asked.

"I'm sure you have it under control there, don't you?"

"I do, but this is a huge case. You sure you don't need to be here?" His boss wasn't acting right. With his political aspirations, he should be all over this case. To get where he wanted to go, he needed to be the face of the operation.

"Handle it, but keep me apprised." Quentin disconnected the call.

It was an enormous opportunity to be trusted with a case of such magnitude. One he would've been ecstatic about a few days ago. But now, his priorities were shifting. An image of Sadie's smile flashed through his mind. There was more for him in this life than his career, and with God at the center, he was certain it would be the right move to stay in Pennsylvania. Make a life here. No more running.

Craig dialed Brian and he answered after one ring. "Find them yet?"

"Not yet, but I have a lead. Care to join me?"

"I'm sure your bosses will have something to say about that."

"They left me in charge."

"In that case, count me in. I'll be there in thirty."

Chapter Twenty-Six

True to his word, Brian arrived in thirty minutes and they reviewed the security footage again together.

Brian tapped Jerome on the shoulder. "Is there a way into the hotel where someone can avoid the cameras completely?"

Jerome pushed his chair back so he could look into Brian's eyes. "Your guy didn't avoid the cameras, so is that relevant?"

"It may be. Yes."

"There is a tunnel that comes up under Element. Many of the staff use it to get from the train station to the building without going outside."

"That's our answer."

"Did you find out what room he was staying in yet?"

Craig shook his head. "Don't have a name yet, but Jerome printed this out with the time stamp. It should help the front desk staff find the reservation.

Brian approached the desk and smiled at the pretty blonde behind the counter. "Think you can help me out?"

The woman looked at Craig as if asking permission.

"He's with me."

"Sure thing."

"This man checked in on December 19th at eleven o'clock at night. Can you check your records and find out what name he checked in under and what room he was in? We're going to need to have a look at his room."

"My manager will have to authorize that."

"That's no problem." Brian tapped a hand against the counter.

"I already talked to Mr. Stapleton. He offered his full cooperation, so I don't think you'll have any trouble getting that authorization."

"Okay, but there is still one tiny problem."

"What's that?"

"We don't have a way to search reservations based on the time they were made."

"That is a problem, isn't it?"

She reached her hand over the counter. "Can I see that picture you have there?"

Craig handed it over for her to inspect.

"I recognize him. I don't remember his first name, but his last name is Carter." She smiled. "I can search by last name." Her eyes lit as she pointed at her screen. "Here it is. Room 613."

"Call your manager for authorization. Then give me a key to that room, please."

CRAIG AND BRIAN STOOD outside of the room with their weapons drawn. With a nod from Craig, Brian inserted the key card and pushed the door open. Craig cleared the main room before entering the bathroom. Brian was right behind him. There huddled in a grimy bathtub sat two women bound and gagged, but alive.

Tears streamed down Brian's face as he reached for his mother. Craig's hand on his shoulder stopped him. "Pictures first. We'll need them later."

"Right."

Craig snapped a few photos from his cell and then he and Brian worked at releasing the women from the ropes that bound them together. From the looks of the indentations in the shower wall, they'd been working together to get someone's attention since they'd been left here.

He lifted his radio. "I'm going to need a bus at Element. 1441 Chestnut Street. Two kidnapping victims in need of medical attention."

Mrs. Kline clung to her son with what little strength she had, and he lifted her easily out of the tub. Craig assisted Mrs. Wright. "You're safe now. We're going to get you to the hospital."

"Matt. He was going after Matt." Her words were raspy. Who knew when they'd been given water last?

"We know."

"Is he...?"

She deserved to know the truth though he hated to be the one to share it. "He's alive. Hospitalized." If there was any justice in the world, he'd be okay, but justice wasn't something they were guaranteed in this lifetime. Sometimes bad things did happen to good people. Not that anyone was truly good. They were all sinful broken people, but Matt was as good as they came. He'd devoted his life to coming up with ways to combat biological warfare. It was a noble calling. And one that came close to costing him his life. Craig wanted to believe he would pull through, even though the evidence told him Matt's survival was unlikely.

Chapter Twenty-Seven

Standing in the doorway of the hospital room, Sadie swiped away tears. Her mother had survived.

Dad pulled a seat up close to the bed and held Mom's hand. It wasn't until Brian called an hour earlier that she consciously realized she hadn't expected them to find their mother alive. Even now, tension slowly ebbed from her muscles, and she expected to collapse from a mixture of relief and exhaustion. Brian approached with bottled water and Snickers bars and tossed her one of each. "Merry Christmas, Sadie."

Spending holidays in the hospital was typical for her since she'd become a nurse, but this situation certainly hadn't been. "Thanks. Right back at you." It wasn't her usual fare, but she couldn't remember the last time she'd eaten something, so she tore open the package and bit into the chocolaty goodness.

"Craig's in the waiting area."

"He is?"

"I don't think I'm the one my best friend is here to support."

She studied his expression. "Are you okay with—"

"Nobody will ever be good enough for my baby sister, but Craig is as close as they come. If you two want to give it a go, I'll be supportive, but don't go telling him that."

Another tear slipped past her lashes.

"Don't get all sappy. Go send him away. There's a biological weapon out there somewhere along with the antidote that can keep it from killing thousands. Craig needs to get to work securing those instead of sitting around here pining over you."

"How do you know about Viper-X?"

"Never heard the name before, but Craig gave me a general idea of what was going on." He smiled. "Now go."

It irked her that Craig shared his case information so freely with her brother when she'd had to pull it out of him, but she quickened her steps as she considered the magnitude of what he was dealing with.

He'd placed her needs ahead of his case. More than once. That had to mean something, right?

When she reached the waiting area, he stood and stuffed his phone into his coat pocket. "How's your mom?"

"She's sleeping." She tilted her head to the side and smiled. "Want to get some fresh air?"

"Sure." Once they were on the sidewalk, she threaded her fingers through his. "Thanks for being here."

"I can't work twenty-four hours a day."

"No, but you do need to sleep."

"I caught a few hours last night."

"Which is why you were fresh enough to find my mother today."

He brushed a hair from her face. "Now that Javier is dead, you should be safe to return home."

"What about Alhad Sharma?"

"Our threat assessment suggests he's either already fled the country or soon will. It's unlikely that you're on his radar."

"That's good news, but if he's gone how will you find the weapon?"

"I don't know." He lifted her hand to his lips and kissed her palm. "Long hours and fervent prayers await."

"You should go. Get some rest before you have to start all over in the morning."

"Are you sending me away?"

"I am."

"Forever?"

"I don't have the strength for that."

He released her hand and grabbed her around the waist, dragging her to himself. "Why is that?"

"You know why."

"I want to hear you say it, Sadie. I need to hear you say the words."

She pushed at his chest. "You've known how I felt about you since my freshman year."

"Your feelings haven't changed?"

"I tried to make them go away. I didn't want to love

you."

"I know. I may not deserve you, but I'm not sorry you didn't give that precious heart to another man." His lips lowered to hers, and he kissed away the years of emptiness she'd felt without him in her life. "It shouldn't have taken me so long to realize you're the only woman for me."

"I won't argue with that."

His thumb brushed over her swollen bottom lip. "I could kiss you all night."

"We don't have time for that. You should go. You have a criminal to stop, and I need to be with my family."

He kissed her again, exploring her mouth with languid movements, taking his sweet time as if they did indeed have all night to spend in each other's arms. Then he took a step back, leaving her off-balance with the suddenness of his withdraw. "I'll call you tomorrow."

"Some maniac made me leave my phone in Danville."

"Would that be the maniac you're in love with?" He winked and reached into his inside coat pocket, pulling out a box. Tossing it to her, he said, "Merry Christmas!"

After he disappeared around the corner, she opened the package. A brand-new iPhone. She was more of an Android girl, but it was the thought that counted. A warmth spread through her chest. Yes, she was in love with him. It was more than the zing of awareness that flitted through her every time he touched her hand. It was their shared history, the way he made her laugh, even the way he worshipped God and put Him foremost in his life. Of course, the way he kissed didn't hurt either.

A slow smile spread as she trotted back inside.

Her feelings for him may have started as a schoolgirl crush, but the more time she spent in adult Craig's presence, the more she was certain he was the man God intended for her. It had always been him. It would always be him.

CRAIG DROPPED TO HIS knees on the side of the hotel bed. "Lord, you know the desires of my heart. If Sadie isn't the one for me, please make that clear to both of us before we go any further." He wanted to make her his wife, but it was sudden. A week ago, he could've honestly said he hadn't thought of her in ages. Now she consumed his thoughts.

His focus needed to remain on the case. The FBI discovered the auction. They hadn't been able to identify what was up for bid, but the timing fit and the price was right. It was Viper-X.

The high bidder appeared to be from China, but he could've bounced his signal from anywhere, so tracking him would be near impossible.

If they could figure out how and when payment would be made and the exchange would happen, they'd have something, but at this point they didn't even know how the buyers learned about the auction. If it was invitation only, and that was likely the case, the person issuing those invitations could be their link back to Dr. Alhad Sharma, the buyer, and an account that would soon have more than fifty million dollars in it.

They knew it was Alhad Sharma selling out his country to the highest bidder, but they needed to track him down and bring him to justice. And they needed to stop a catastrophe before it happened.

Chapter Twenty-Eight

Sadie lay beneath the quilt in her childhood bedroom. She'd opened her Bible and read from Romans before extinguishing the light. A verse about all things working together for good stuck in her mind. None of what had happened in the past week felt like good, but it had brought Craig back into her life and reminded her to put her trust in God and not herself. Maybe the verse didn't mean all things would be sunshine and rainbows. Could it be like a refiner's fire, where raw metal goes in and impurities are burned off? Maybe that's the good. The trials burn off the rough edges and a person comes through better than they were before they went through the difficulties. It was a nice thought. Another verse in the Bible called God the potter and His people the clay. The trouble with her was she kept trying to mold and shape herself instead of letting the Master have the control.

Giving up the reins of her own life wasn't easy. She sat up, flipped the light back on, and opened her nightstand to pull out some old photographs. Craig and Brian after a football game. Craig and Brian with a couple of cheerleaders. Craig in the pool. He'd been splashing her, but she didn't want her camera wet, so she'd snapped the photo and gone back inside. Yes, they'd done their share of flirting, but he'd never let it go beyond that despite knowing how much she cared for him. Why?

What had changed between them to make him see her in a new light? Was Craig God's will for her? Did he love her? He'd told her he needed to hear her say the words, but he hadn't repeated them back to her. She loved him so much it made her chest ache. She had for as long as she could remember, but she'd moved on with her life. Now he was back.

Was she destined to cry herself to sleep for months again? Would he leave again once he'd completed his case and saved the day? She didn't want to stand in the way of his career, but she didn't want to stop being a nurse to follow him. Wasn't that the path God had led her on? Would He have done so only to ask her to follow a man around the country? Was that something she wanted? There were so many questions ping-ponging around in her head. Then the words of the Lord replayed in her mind. Be still and know that I am God. She knew it was from Psalm 46, but she couldn't recall the verse number.

Here she was trying to take over again. All she needed to do was be still and trust that God had her covered. It was simple, but it wasn't easy.

ALHAD GRINNED LIKE A fool. The auction had gone better than anticipated. He pulled Rajesh into a hug. "Thank you for taking care of my transportation problem, Rajesh." The private jet had a passenger manifest, but security was lax and he'd have no trouble passing it using one of his fake identities.

"You know I don't go by my birth name."

"But you will, won't you? Once we relocate?"

His brother shook his head vehemently. "No. I'll keep my name."

"Suit yourself."

Rajesh rubbed his chin, a look of consternation crossing his features. "Javier's dead, but I'm concerned about who he might've shared intel with."

"Don't be. He didn't open his mouth."

"How can you be so sure, and why did you involve that hair-brained fool to begin with?"

"His involvement threw suspicion off you. If he hadn't been so clumsy with his maneuvering, the government would've discovered you."

"Doubt it. I know how to cover my tracks." A sly smile spread across his face. "I'm good at what I do."

"Yes, you are. At least you were until you let that Madison woman live. At this point they haven't managed to connect you to me, but it's only a matter of time if they look hard enough. So, we need to give them somewhere else to look at least until you arrive in Tunisia. There is no extradition treaty between them and the US, so we'll both be safe there."

The other man glanced at his cell screen, probably checking to see if the funds transfer went through. "I'll see you there on January 1st, little brother."

Alhad put a hand over his heart. "Until then." They'd both been adopted into American families as children, but they'd stayed in touch. His older sibling was the only biological family he had left. But now that they were wealthy beyond their wildest dreams, they could both settle down with nice girls, get married, and have lots of babies. Family of his own. A lifelong dream, and it would finally be realized.

A few more days, and he'd have everything he ever desired.

CRAIG WALKED INTO THE conference room.

Lisa was reclined in her chair fiddling with her phone, and Joel was bent over the conference table filling out paperwork.

"Hey."

"You have something new, boss?" Joel asked.

"Quentin's the boss."

"Left you in charge, didn't he?" Lisa asked.

"I guess he did." He plopped into a seat at the head of the table. "I can't reach him. That's unusual."

Murmurs of agreement answered him.

"The FBI thinks they found the auction we were expecting. It finished at 5 a.m.," Craig said.

"Today? On Christmas Day?"

"That's right."

Lisa uncrossed her legs and leaned away from the table. "Viper-X will probably be deployed soon."

Craig cleared his throat. "I'm thinking the same thing. I'd like to get Quentin's permission to form a task force with the FBI. New Year's celebrations will be happening all over the country next week. If they're looking for a target, I'm guessing they'll think big. Times Square. Or if they prefer less security, they might choose a place like Miami."

Joel bounced his pen between his forefinger and middle finger. "Or Philadelphia, Chicago, New Orleans. There are too many soft targets to list. Thousands of possibilities. They wouldn't pick the most obvious option."

"That only eliminates Times Square. *If* you're right about how they think," Lisa said.

"I don't have the answer, but we need to find that weapon before it kills hundreds or even thousands of innocent civilians," Craig said.

"I'm with you, boss, but how do we do that?" Lisa lifted a brow.

"I have no idea." His only answer was prayer. And lots of it.

Craig pushed his chair back and stood. "Go home and be with your families tonight. There is no reason for us to stay in Philly. We've done as much as we can here.

We'll follow the leads from our home computers until we figure out where to go to stop this thing. Touch base with me tomorrow morning, and I'll expect both of you to be available for a video conference Friday at 8 a.m. I should be in Washington DC by then."

"Yes, sir." Lisa jumped to her feet and saluted. "Talk to you tomorrow." She flew out the door.

Joel shook his head and smiled. "That girl is something else."

Was there something between the two of them, or was Craig seeing things where they didn't exist because of his own romantic notions toward a certain tiny brunette? Hard to say, but he was taking the rest of the day off and hoped to spend Christmas with the woman he loved. Lord help him, he did love her.

Chapter Twenty-Nine

Craig arrived in Ridley with his bag packed. When he knocked on the front door, his mother ushered him inside. "What are you knocking for? This will always be your home."

"There was an abduction next door a few days ago, I didn't want to take the chance Dad would mistake me for an intruder and shoot me."

His father laughed. "We just got home from visiting Harry and Eleanor. Sounds like quite an ordeal she went through."

"I'm glad they discharged her, so she could spend Christmas at home with her family," Mom said.

"I'm going to head over there in a few, but I wanted to see if I could stay here tonight, so I can hang out a little later with Sadie."

"You and Sadie, huh?" His father grinned.

"I always thought you two would make a nice couple."

"I haven't given her a ring, Mom. We went on a couple of dates, and one of those was interrupted, so it's a little soon to be ordering the wedding cake."

"Pssh. When you know, you know." She smacked him with the back of her hand. "You two will give me beautiful grandchildren."

He shook his head. "This is why I don't tell you things. The next thing I know, you'll be at Carters picking out onesies."

His dad chuckled. "She will, too. Go on and take your things up to your room. I imagine the Kline girl saw you pull into the drive, and if you don't want to hurt her feelings, you'd best get over there."

"What about Christmas dinner?"

"I'm sure Sadie will feed you." His father tapped his watch.

"We ate an hour ago, but there are plenty of leftovers. I'll fix you a plate and stick it in the fridge, so you can have it when you get back."

"He won't need them. That girl was raised right. She'll feed him."

SADIE ANSWERED THE DOOR. Instead of joining her inside, he tugged her outside to join him. She shivered in the cool night air. He drew her to himself. "I think I can ward off that chill."

His lips claimed hers with a possessive passion, and she had to admit he wasn't wrong. He warmed her through and through with his kisses. "My parents are probably wondering what happened to us."

"They were young once. I'm sure they can guess."

"I'm glad you came."

"Me too. I couldn't bear the thought of working through Christmas instead of celebrating it with you."

"Then come inside with me." She laced their fingers together and tugged him toward the door.

"In a minute. I need a few minutes alone with you first." He lowered his mouth to hers once more. In her arms, he could forget about the threat facing the country. Being close to her was intoxicating.

A smile lit her eyes. "I promise we'll get some alone time after you say 'hi' to my parents."

He held the door, and she scurried inside, dragging him along behind her.

When Sadie released him, he gave Mrs. Kline a gentle hug. "I'm glad they kicked you loose from the hospital so you could be with family today."

"Me too. Just wish I hadn't missed Christmas Eve service."

Craig squeezed her hand. "I get that. Me too."

"Dad read the Christmas story from Luke before dinner. It's one of my favorite traditions." Sadie tapped a nail on the Bible on the table beside the couch.

"Sorry I missed it."

Brian breezed through the door. "I know I'm late. Did you save me some food?" He took a step back when he spotted Craig standing beside Sadie. "Didn't expect you here."

Craig rested a hand on her shoulder. "I think you can expect to see more of me."

Sadie looked up at him and smiled. That was what she'd been longing to hear. That she wasn't a distraction or diversion to keep his mind off the realities of the case, but that he cared enough to stick around.

"I hope so, man." Brian headed into the dining room and Craig followed. She swallowed down the urge to follow, letting them have a few minutes alone.

CRAIG LEANED AGAINST THE door jamb and tossed his keys in an arc, eyes fixed on Brian, while he waited for him to share whatever was on his mind. His stomach growled from the apple and cinnamon aroma filling the house.

"You know she pined over you for years."

"I never led her on."

"I know. She was off-limits because she was my sister and you didn't want to ruin our friendship."

"That's right."

Brian scowled. "You're willing to take that chance now?"

"She's an adult, far from a little girl who needs her over-protective older brother to step in and interfere in her relationships."

A muscle jumped in Brian's jaw. "I'll never stop wanting to cause harm to someone who hurts my sister."

"If I wasn't serious about her, I wouldn't be here right now."

"All right, then. Let's eat. They hid the food, but I'll find it."

Turned out the food wasn't hidden all that well—it was packaged neatly in labeled containers. They each microwaved a bowl and took a seat at the dining room table. Sadie lingered in the doorway, watching them. "I was going to offer to make you a plate, but it looks like Brian beat me to it."

Craig patted the seat beside him. "Come sit with me." He took a forkful of sweet potatoes, savoring the sweet molasses flavor before swallowing.

She did as he asked, and he tugged her chair closer before giving her knee a pat.

Brian scarfed his food down and stood. "I'll see you guys later. I'm going to give Mom and Dad their Christmas present."

Sadie lifted a brow. "What did you get them this year?"

"A cruise."

"Where to?"

"Alaska."

"Well, I have no chance of winning Christmas this year, do I?"

"You never do, sis." He winked and made his exit.

"Is he always so extravagant with his gifts for your parents?"

She nodded. "It's less a competition between us and more of a competition he holds with himself. He thinks he needs to outdo his previous gift each and every year."

"What was last year's gift?"

"Two weeks in Kauai."

"And the year before?"

"That might've been a Caribbean cruise."

"Hmm." He smiled. "Know what I'm thinking?"

"That you want to adopt my brother?"

"Exactly." Laughing, he pushed his plate away. He stood and pulled her into his arms, reveling in the smell of peaches and cream that was all her. Whatever that shampoo was, he'd never known anyone else to use it. "We need a do-over for our second date. Can this count?"

"Absolutely."

"And what about a third date?" His lips lowered to within inches of hers, their breath mingling, as he spoke against her mouth. "Will you let me take you out again?"

She kissed him, her eyes sparkling. "Do you really need to ask?"

Chapter Thirty

Madison unlocked the door, and Brian held it open. Sadie stepped inside and made a slow circle, taking in the disarray. When they'd left, their apartment was a cozy sanctuary. No more. The table was turned over, a lamp lay shattered, and an icy breeze blew in through a broken window, bringing the scent of a coming snowstorm with it.

Brian wrapped an arm around her shoulders and pulled her closer. "I'll get that window replaced tomorrow. In the meantime, I'll board it over for you."

"I don't have plywood." She knelt and lifted her Bible from the rubble, brushing bits of broken glass from the soft calfskin cover.

"I'll get some. We passed a Kohl's Hardware store. I'm sure they'll have something."

Madison swiveled on her heel and strode out the door without a word.

"Do you mind if I follow her?" Brian asked.

Sadie hugged God's word to her chest. "No, go ahead. She needs you more than I do." She exhaled, knowing it was true. Sadie had the Lord—Madison did not. Her hope wasn't built on something solid, so when tragedy struck, she was left cold.

The words of a hymn echoed in her memories.

The Bible stands tho' the hills may tumble,It will firmly stand when the earth shall crumble;I will plant my feet on its firm foundation,For the Bible stands.

Despite everything, God's words remained a lamp unto her feet, but they wouldn't fade away or shatter. The Bible would light her path through every circumstance, good or bad, if she let it. The Holy Spirit provided the oil to keep the lamp burning and guide her along her journey.

Brian and Madison returned, and Sadie's eyebrows raised at the sight of her brother with his arm around her roommate. No doubt it was simple platonic comfort, but it felt strange to see the two of them in that position.

Sadie brushed a spot on the couch clean for them to sit. "I'll get this mess cleaned up."

BRIAN STOOD. "I SHOULD get going."

"Thanks for the ride home," Madison said. She glanced his way and then shifted her attention to the street below. Whatever had happened during the few hours between those men showing up at the lab and

Craig rescuing her, she wasn't interested in talking about it. Yesterday was the first time she'd left Matt's side. He was in a coma, and the doctors weren't optimistic about him coming out of it.

Sadie met Brian at the apartment door. The landing at the top of the stairs was dark, the bulb having burned out weeks earlier. She rested a hand on the sleeve of his smooth leather jacket and breathed in the familiar scent of his cologne. It usually bothered her, but today it brought comfort. "I'll walk you down."

Their steps echoed in the empty stairwell as they descended.

He lingered at the bottom of the stairs. "Think she'll be all right?"

"Eventually." Sadie pulled her soft cotton cardigan around herself to ward off the chill. "Her heart is broken. They talked about getting married. Having a family."

"He may recover."

"We're nurses in the emergency department. With all we've seen, we know when hope is slim."

"Our God works miracles, Sadie."

"He does. And sometimes, he doesn't choose to save someone. We need to be okay with whatever His will is. Madison isn't. Her relationship with the Lord is on shaky ground. Has been since she lost her parents."

"I'll have to ask her about them some time."

"She'd like that." She hugged him. "Thanks for the lift. I hate that you have to go already."

"I don't want to stay away from Mom long. Dad can't be with her all the time, so we're planning to take turns at the house."

"What about your dog?"

"I brought Princess to Mom and Dad's house. It'll be a miracle if Mom lets me take her home with me."

"I'm glad you're there with them. I wish I could be closer."

"You can, sis. There are jobs at the local hospitals."

"Maybe I'll look into them. I thought it would be nice to be out here in the country, but I miss family."

"We miss you." He hesitated at the door. "Call if you need anything. And let me know if Craig does anything to make you cry."

"Sure thing." She smiled.

He left, turning to give her one last wave before firing up his car and heading back to Delaware County.

BRIAN HAD DRIVEN SADIE and Madison back to Danville Thursday afternoon, which left Craig free to wrap things up in Philadelphia. He'd driven himself back from Central Pennsylvania early that morning before their scheduled Friday video conference.

The meeting had concluded without incident, but nobody had spoken to Quentin since Tuesday, and Craig was worried. Had their perp somehow gotten to him? He'd checked with Quentin's secretary only to be told he was taking some time off. It wasn't like him to bail in the middle of a case. Craig had only been with the agency for a year, but he and Quentin worked together enough for him to get a good understanding of the other man. And truth be told, he was a control-freak. He didn't like handing over the reins to anyone else. It was out of character.

The joint task-force with the FBI had been approved by the higher-ups and would take place first thing Friday in the nation's capital. Craig took out a couple of suits to pack and his mind played back Sadie's words about him wearing a nondescript suit and driving a nondescript car. He inspected the suit and chuckled before hanging it in his garment bag. It fit her description. Nothing about him would stand out in the dull charcoal suit. He grabbed a dark tie, but then snagged a red one, too. Not something he would normally wear, but it was the Christmas season, and there was nothing wrong with a touch of color.

Seemed Sadie was affecting his behavior. He sat on the edge of the bed and pulled his Bible into his lap. It had been more than a week since he'd opened it. Life could get hectic, but making time for the Lord needed to be a priority. Leaning back against the headrest, he opened to the gospel of John and started reading.

Later that night, before hitting the road, he dialed Sadie's number. It took three rings for her to answer.

"Hey."

"Hi. You busy?"

"Just arriving at work. I have a twelve-hour shift."

"Did you get enough rest?"

She yawned. "As much as can be expected after the week we've had."

"I have to go to Washington on business."

"When do you leave?"

"Tonight."

"Do you know when you'll be back?"

"I don't."

"Is this about the stolen weapon?"

"It is."

"I'll be praying for you."

His heart stopped. No woman had ever said those words to him before. They'd wished him good luck. Told him they'd miss him. Even offered to give him something to remember them by, so he'd want to return to them, but this was a first. This woman cared about him enough to pray for him. And it was the most beautiful thing he'd ever experienced.

"Craig?"

"I'm here. Thank you for praying. You don't know how much that means to me."

"I wish I could be there with you as a support system, but since I don't think the government wants me following you around, we'll have to settle for phone calls. Call when you can, okay?"

"I will." He paused. "And Sadie?"

"Yeah?"

He wanted to say the three little words that he knew she also needed to hear, but he couldn't bring himself to say them over the phone. She deserved to hear them in person. "I'll see you soon."

CHAPTER THIRTY-ONE

CRAIG GLANCED OUT THE window of Quentin Finnegan's office. Quentin had left without getting the paperwork for their current investigation in order. The government was trying to go paperless, but since most case officers couldn't read thousands of pages of paperwork on a computer screen, they wound up printing the same information dozens of times only to shred it when they were through with a case.

It seemed Quentin had already done some shredding. And taken whatever was left with him. Craig printed out the case files and sat at his desk poring over them, the acrid aroma of stale coffee and the incessant whir of the printer his only companions since everyone else had left for the day.

He read through the paperwork for Viper-X, the biological weapon Alhad Sharma had developed in New Mexico. Most of it was over Craig's head. A shame Matt wasn't conscious and able to explain it to him.

When he got to the records for the mission budget, he set them atop his to-be-read pile, but kept his hand on the folder. He hated budgets, but if this was his operation, he needed to know what resources he had available. Frowning at it, he set the folder in front of him and opened it. The budget was larger than he'd expected. Granted, it was a high-risk matter, but he hadn't expected the budget to reflect that as stingy as Quentin was with resources.

Most of the line items related to him and his unit, so there was little he didn't already know about. As he scanned the second page, his finger landed on a charge for an identity for Joel. Joel hadn't needed a cover on this job. It didn't add up. Unless Quentin considered sending him undercover, but he didn't usually assign men under Craig's authority without running it by him first.

The name on the cover, Alec Stewart, stood out. Odd. Sharma used the name Adam to check into the hospital in Danville. Adam Smith. Same initials. Could be a coincidence. An odd one if it was.

On the next page, he found several payments to a transportation logistics company named Gaylord Transportation that totaled three hundred twenty-five thousand. Why would Quentin authorize those payments? He'd have to look into that company and find out what they were all about. That kind of money was enough to pay for brand new high-end armored SUVs for the unit, yet he'd been forced to get the cheapest rental possible for his witnesses, and he was driving a hand-me down loaner from another department. Something was off.

He'd been convinced that Quentin was having medical problems or something in his personal life was interfering with work, but this didn't smell right. Craig stood and pressed the speed dial button on his cell phone. Wally was the only person in this town he trusted. It was time for a face-to-face with his old friend.

SADIE CHATTED WITH CALEB, a young patient with possible appendicitis about his stuffed sheep. His mother stood nearby worrying her bottom lip and twisting her shirt with both hands. In between winces of pain, Caleb shared all about the Squishmallow he squeezed to his chest.

"What's his name?"

"Harry."

"My dad's name is Harry. That's a good strong name. Did you name him yourself?"

He let out another anguished groan before nodding. She pressed on different areas of his abdomen. The doctor would need to order a scan, but it looked like the poor child would need surgery.

"We're going to take you in for a scan of your belly. Miss Ellen will be in to get you soon."

Sadie gestured for the mother to speak with her outside of the room. "The doctor will be in shortly, but I expect we'll be taking him in for a CT scan."

After taking a minute to calm the frantic mother, Sadie

wrote her notes in the chart and moved on to the next room. A busy night filled with the usual mishaps from teens attempting to capture stunts for their social media channels to kitchen and construction accidents. The week between Christmas and New Year's was no less eventful than usual. On the bright side, her shift was ending, so soon she'd be curled up under her comforter dreaming about when she'd see Craig again.

Madison draped an arm around her shoulders. "How are you holding up?"

"Dead on my feet." Sadie locked eyes with her friend. "You?"

"Same." But despite her friend's words, nothing was the same for her. She hadn't been eating or sleeping, and she was dodging calls from Matt's mom. Everyone responded differently to tragedy, and Sadie couldn't say how she would react if the man she loved was languishing in a coma, but she hoped that her faith would give her the strength to get through it. Madison's experiences with religion had left her wary of anything associated with it. And as much as Sadie wanted to help her find the inner peace that came from a relationship with Jesus, she couldn't force her to accept the truth of God's word. In the meantime, she would trust that the Holy Spirit was drawing her friend closer to Him with each passing day.

CRAIG SAT ON THE dock overlooking the Potomac and watched as chunks of ice floated by. A man walked up and kicked his side.

"Careful. If I hadn't known it was you, I might've taken you out."

"You might have the skills to kill me with your bare hands, but you're not the type to do so without just cause." Wally grinned. "You forget how well I know you and your faithful Friend Jesus."

"Sit down." He motioned to the empty space beside him on the dock.

Wally lowered himself onto the concrete and frowned. "I'm getting too old for sitting on the hard ground."

"You're thirty. That's not old."

"What's made you paranoid enough to request a clandestine meeting?"

"I think my boss is involved in my case."

"I should hope so."

"On the wrong side of the law."

"Quentin Finnegan? Seriously?"

Craig pulled the wad of papers from the pocket of his wool coat and passed them to Wally. "The highlighted sections concern me."

"Who is Joel Bergen?"

"One of my guys in Homeland. The one who took the fatal shot on Javier Garcia on my orders."

"You think he's in on this?"

Craig sighed. "I don't know. Right now, you're the only one working for Uncle Sam that I trust."

"What are these financial transactions?"

"I don't know. I went to the library and tried to research them. They don't seem to exist."

"Shell companies?"

"The addresses seem to indicate that."

"Let me look them up."

"Can you do so without sending up an alert to Homeland?"

"Come on now, you know how our agencies hate sharing information with each other."

Craig laughed. "I do." He remained silent while Wally tapped away on his phone.

"I have a name."

"Yeah?"

"Adam Stevenson. He's linked to a number of other shell companies as well."

"Now that's interesting. The name of the identity created for Joel was Alec Stewart."

"A.S." Wally picked at his fingernails. "Could be coincidence."

"Maybe, but the name of the doctor we're after is Alhad Sharma."

"Not a coincidence, then."

"More like Quentin toying with us, knowing he'd be long gone by the time we found it."

"I think I may know someone who can help."

"I'm not crazy about involving anyone else."

"You won't mind bringing him in. Dante Reyes is in town."

"What's he doing here? Thought he was deployed."

"Didn't re-up."

"I had no idea he'd left the Navy."

"He may or may not be with a three-letter agency that doesn't like to divulge secrets. We worked on a case together a couple of months ago, and he shared the location of his safe house."

"For such a time as this." Dante had led Craig to the Lord when he'd been bleeding out in a chopper. It was a miracle he'd survived, and there was no man on earth he trusted more.

"Exactly. I'll call and have him meet us there."

Chapter Thirty-Two

Craig sat in the passenger seat watching glistening evergreens roll by while Wally drove them to Dante's place. He'd only managed to talk with Sadie once since he'd arrived in Washington as they kept missing each other. He tapped his phone against his leg. She'd be getting home about now, but it was late. Too late to call.

"What's eating you? This thing with Quentin?"

"You'd think so, wouldn't you? Threat of a deadly and highly contagious biological weapon expected to be deployed at a New Year's event somewhere in the United States. Target Unknown." He sighed and leaned back against the headrest. "Yes, it's bothering me. Quite a bit. But so is a woman."

Wally laughed. "Women have a way of turning us inside out. That's for certain. What about this particular one has you squirming in your seat like you have a scorpion under your rear?"

"If there was a scorpion, I'd jump out of a moving vehicle."

"You're deflecting."

"She's literally the girl next door. We decided to try a relationship between us, but I'm here and she's in Central Pennsylvania. We can't even manage to reach each other on the phone."

"What's she do for a living?"

"Emergency department nurse."

"Ah. Serious job."

"Yep."

"You planning to go back there?"

"I don't know. Homeland Security could place me anywhere."

"Will she follow?"

"I think so, but is it fair to ask her to give up everything she's worked so hard for?"

"You don't have to do that. She can work as a nurse wherever the two of you settle."

"We aren't at the exchanging rings stage yet. This is new."

"How long have you known her?"

"Since the day they brought her home from the hospital."

"If you don't know by now..."

"Yes. We know each other, but we don't know if this will work."

"Dating someone you know that well isn't going to help you get to know her better. If you don't want to live without the girl, put a ring on her finger."

"How much farther to Dante's place?" Craig glanced at his watch.

"There you go changing the subject again." Wally wound his way down a narrow tree-lined drive that was practically invisible and rolled to a stop in a circular drive. "We're here." Wally switched off the car and slipped out.

Craig stepped out of the vehicle, scanning surroundings barely visible beneath the waning crescent moon. The isolated location was silent. Eerie. He took a deep breath of crisp, cool pine-scented air. "Ready for this?"

"Let's do it." Wally led the way up the stone path leading to the remote log cabin.

CRAIG STOOD BACK AS Wally entered the security code Dante had given him. The heavy steel door swung open on its own, and he followed Wally inside.

It was a den in what looked like a hunter's cabin. The head of a twelve-point buck was mounted on the wall and there was a plaid couch and matching chair.

Wally sank into the chair, leaving the couch for Craig. "This is as far as we go until Dante arrives. The door leading into his inner sanctum has a biometric lock.

"This place doesn't look like Dante's style."

"That's kind of the point, isn't it?"

Craig yawned. "I suppose so."

"Am I keeping you up?"

"Haven't had much sleep since Sadie's mother was

kidnapped."

"Brian's sister Sadie is your girl next door?"

"Yes." He yawned again.

"You're not going to be much use in stopping this biological attack if you don't grab a few hours shut-eye from time to time."

"Don't I know it?"

The low rumble of an approaching vehicle had them both on alert. Wally looked out the window. "It's Dante's Jeep."

Two minutes later, Dante joined them in his den. "Sorry about the primitive accommodations, boys. It was the best I could offer on short notice. While you're here, we'll get you loaded into the security system in case you need to come back for any reason."

"That would be stellar, though I hope I won't need it." Craig rubbed the back of his neck, releasing some of the tension gathered there.

Dante looked into the eye of the buck on the wall and a scanner popped out of a log beside it. He placed his palm on it, and a bookshelf on the opposite wall swung open. "Welcome to my abode, men."

They stepped into a small room with a set of stairs leading down to an enormous below-ground apartment with every modern convenience. Craig wandered around, baffled that a space so large could exist below a one-room cabin.

Once they'd all taken their seats in the sleek living area, Dante locked eyes with Craig. "What has you seeking the assistance of your SEAL brothers, Chief?"

"How much did Wally share?"

"Not much. Just that you suspected someone in your organization of treason."

"That about sums it up." Craig pressed his palms against his eyes a moment then dropped his hands to his knees. "It's been a long couple of weeks. First I got tapped to keep an eye on a scientist who was working on an antidote for Viper-X."

"And that is?"

"A biological weapon designed to be administered as a mist. It can be sprayed over a large area in seconds. It's highly contagious and deadly."

"Is there a reason we need this now?"

"Unfortunately, yes. The doctor developing the weapon stole it. They have since auctioned it off to the highest bidder."

Dante sat forward. "Go on."

Craig stood and paced the length of the room. "Dr. Matt Wright, the researcher who came up with the antidote was kidnapped right under our agency's nose while Quentin and I and several others from my agency were dealing with a distraction. We thought it was a lead on our culprit, but he set up the diversion so he would have easier access to the doctor."

"How did he get past security?"

"We haven't figured that out. When we went to review the surveillance from the lab, it had been erased. It was a direct feed to Homeland, so that made me wonder if it could be an inside man."

"Someone on your team?"

"At first I suspected Joel, but the more I dig into it, the more I think it's possible my boss was setting him up to take the fall as the inside man."

"I'm surprised he didn't set you up."

"Would've been harder. If I wasn't with my team at HSD, I was with the Ridley PD or the FBI." He twisted a string on his sweater. "Might've involved Fred and then killed him to cover his tracks."

"You lost a guy?"

"At the lab when Matt Wright was kidnapped."

"So, he could've been working with your boss, or he may have become suspicious of him."

"I wondered that, too. We may never know which it was."

"Still, none of that explains what you wanted me to look into."

"I need someone who can look into my boss discreetly."

"What do you want to know?"

"Everything you can dredge up."

"That may take some time, but I can give you the basics without much trouble."

"Let's start there."

Dante pressed a button on a remote, and the coffee table opened, revealing a touchscreen computer. "What's this guy's name?"

"Quentin Finnegan. Field Operations Supervisor."

"Here we are. Born in India to Unmesh and Chithra Sharma. Adopted by an American family at the age of five. His name was Rajesh until his new parents changed it to Quentin."

Craig sat up, his spine straightening. "Sharma?"

"Yes. He also had a brother who was adopted around the same time. His brother's family kept his birth name. Alhad."

"You have to be kidding me."

"What?"

"The doctor who developed Viper-X is Alhad Sharma."

"Seems your suspicions about your boss may be spot on. Now you have to find a way to prove he's involved in his brother's dealings."

"The fact that he didn't hand this case off to a different unit is proof enough for me."

"It won't quite cut it in a court of law."

"No, but his sudden disappearance, the shady financials in the case file, combined with his personal connection to the case, should be all I need to bring him down. If I can find him."

Dante grinned. "I may be able to help with that." His eyebrows wiggled up and down. "We recently got access to a new toy."

"What's that?"

"It's our eye in the sky. We call it Project Sentinel. It's an advanced AI-driven surveillance and intelligence analysis system that assists us in our missions."

Craig glanced around the impressive safe house once

again. "I guess I don't need to ask which three letter agency you work for these days."

Dante laughed. "You weren't the only SEAL in our platoon worth recruiting."

"Looks to me like you've done rather well for yourself." Craig frowned. "I hope the CIA knows your worth."

Dante waved him off. "Let's find your supervisor."

Chapter Thirty-Three

Craig stood over Dante's shoulder as he worked. He'd given him a quick overview of the features included in Project Sentinel, and now he was seeing them in action. It had facial recognition enhancement, predictive threat analysis, language decoding and analysis, and more. The software could do some real good if used properly, but if misused, it could be a powerful threat. And most things created with good intentions eventually fell into the hands of those who would misuse it for nefarious purposes.

"Finding anything?"

"Does Sharma count?"

"You found Alhad Sharma or his brother?"

"Let's call your former boss Finnegan, to avoid any confusion."

"He's still my boss. He hasn't been removed from his position yet."

"As far as the three of us are concerned, you no longer answer to him."

"True."

"This is what I found. A private jet set to leave from the New Castle Airport in Wilmington, Delaware. It was booked by a man whose facial features match that of your rogue doctor. It's under the identity Abram Solino. Final destination—Tunisia."

"So that we can't extradite. I need that jet locked down."

Dante punched a few keys. "Done."

"Seriously? How do you have that kind of power? Your agency isn't even supposed to be operating in the US."

"What the people do not know, doesn't hurt them, right?"

"You sure you're the same man who led me to Christ?"

"Just repeating the company line. We probably shouldn't have this kind of technology at our fingertips, but the fact is, we do. I think there is good reason why law enforcement needs warrants, but if having the power to shut down a jet may help stop a terrorist attack, who am I to complain?"

"Fair enough. We'll chalk it up as a gray area for now."

"Works for me."

"When is his flight due to take off?"

"Three hours. The jet is in Delaware. Let's go grab him."

"Shall we fly?"

"No. We'll drive, by the time we clear security, it'll be faster."

Dante grinned. "No, it won't."

"I think we've explored enough gray area for one day. Let's drive."

"Have it your way."

Wally frowned. "I was looking forward to the chance to fly in style."

Dante chuckled. "If Craig's driving, I guarantee you'll be flying. He's a stickler for most rules, but he doesn't mind pushing past the speed limit."

Wally punched Craig playfully in the arm. "You should pray about that. I think God can help you control that lead foot of yours."

"I get it from my grandmother."

Dante did a double-take. "You what?"

Craig shrugged.

THEY PARKED AT NEW Castle Airport and headed around to NuWave Jet Charters. Wally took over for the pilot, and Dante took the place of the man at the desk. Craig had Lisa Harper meet him at the airport and take the pilot and desk clerk for a drive to the local HSI field office in Wilmington. He was a little leery trusting anyone from his team, but if anyone else inside the department was helping Quentin Finnegan, Craig was certain it wasn't Lisa Harper. And since her parents lived outside of Wilmington, she was the closest member of his team.

He'd never personally met Alhad Sharma, so he didn't think his presence would raise any flags, but there was a slim chance Finnegan would show up, so Craig stayed out of sight in the back of the plane.

Right on time, Dante led a man to the steps and Wally went out to greet him. "Welcome, are you looking forward to your flight, Mr. Solino?"

"Yes. I'm sure I'll sleep through most of it." He handed his bag to Dante, and Craig reached out with the cuffs. "Alhad Sharma, you're under arrest for espionage, economic espionage, violations of the Biological Weapons Anti-Terrorism Act, and conspiracy to commit offenses against the United States. You have the right to remain silent. Anything you say can and will be used against you in a court of law. You have the right to an attorney. If you cannot afford an attorney, one will be provided for you." Craig grinned. "Do you understand these rights?"

"I'm not the man you're looking for. I'm Abram Solino. Check my passport. It's in the outer pocket of my bag."

Wally laughed and pointed to himself. "FBI." Then he pointed to Dante who had joined them on the plane as Craig was reading Sharma his rights. "He's CIA." And lastly, he motioned to Craig. "He's HSI."

"In other words, we know who you are. Craig, you want me to have a go at him? I'm sure he's heard of our enhanced interrogation methods. It'll be fun."

"I think Homeland Security will fight to keep this one, since he was assisted by one of our own."

Craig watched Sharma's face fall at the mention of his brother. Up until that moment, he didn't realize the severity of his situation. Now he knew his brother wouldn't be able to save him.

"Until Finnegan is officially relieved of his duties, it might be best to let the FBI take custody," Wally said.

As much as Craig hated the idea of giving him up, Wally was right. They couldn't take the chance that Finnegan would manage to free him. They needed to get their intel to the higher-ups, revoke Finnegan's clearances, and issue a warrant for his arrest. "Fine. Take him."

Chapter Thirty-Four

Craig returned to Washington and called Sadie before hitting the sack. Voicemail. He left a message for her to call no matter what time she got in. They hadn't talked in days, and it was killing him. He'd never felt more needy.

He frowned and called Brian. "Hey."

"What's up, man?"

"Heard from your sister recently?"

Brian chuckled. "Trouble in paradise already?"

"Don't make me drive to Ridley and knock you around."

"Sadie called a few hours ago on her meal break to check on Mom."

"You talked to her? She's okay?"

"She's fine. Didn't mention you."

"I've called a few times, but we keep missing each other."

"She ever tell you about the apartment?"

"What about it?"

"When I took her home, we found it ransacked."

Craig sucked in a breath. When he'd sent Sadie home, he'd believed she would be safe. "That's unexpected. Do you think she's safe there?"

"My guess would be that Javier Garcia was responsible. It probably happened before he got Mom. If I had to guess, I would say he initially wanted Madison, but you already had her out of the picture, Sadie was gone, too, so our mom was the low-hanging fruit. Easy pickings that would get Matt's attention."

"I hate that she went through that."

"Me too, but now that Garcia is out of the picture, Sadie should be safe."

"We got Sharma a couple of hours ago."

"The guy who designed Viper-X?"

"FBI has him in custody. We have another suspect who was involved in this with him, but that situation is complicated and can't be resolved tonight."

"What's complicated about it?"

"His co-conspirator is my boss—Finnegan."

"You're kidding."

"Wish I was."

"Will he come after you?"

"Doubt it. He shouldn't have any reason to bother. The two of them already sold Viper-X to the Chinese government, or at least that's what it looks like to my buddy in the CIA. Money is in offshore accounts. Getting to it will be near impossible. If he's smart, he's gone."

"Buddy in the CIA. When did you get friends in high

places, huh?"

"And I didn't even know about his job until last night, but yeah. He's going places."

"I should've gotten myself one of them fancy jobs with the fancy titles."

"You have it made right where you are. A good job. Close to your loved ones. I think I'd switch places with you."

"Dad would hire you on in a heartbeat if you ever want to come on home."

He leaned his head back against the headboard, Wally's words 'if you know, you know' replaying themselves. He did know, and he wouldn't drag his feet and take the chance of losing Sadie to another man. "I may need him to hire me if your sister will have me."

"You two are that serious already?"

"Brian, I've known her all her life, what more is there for us to know about each other? We have the luxury of skipping the whole 'getting to know you' stage. I plan to ask your father's permission before I propose, but I'm going to marry her."

"That's enough bombshells for one conversation, Craig."

"Sorry, I'm exhausted and I talk too much when I'm overtired."

"You'd better treat my sister well."

"I plan to treat her like a princess." Or a ballerina. She'd always be his little ballerina. He didn't care how young she was when she quit dancing, he'd seen her dancing well into her teens when she thought nobody was watching. Her movements were graceful, and her face beamed with her love for dance. It was a shame she'd given it up. Maybe the two of them could take up ballroom dancing together. Anything to see that smile on her face once more.

SADIE LOCKED THE APARTMENT door and scrambled down the steps, checking her phone screen as she approached the outer door. Two missed calls from Craig and one from Brian. She didn't have time to call them back right now.

She needed to get to work to cover someone else's shift. Doing so wouldn't bother her so much if it wasn't for the coworkers who simply called out when they didn't feel like showing up. Legitimate reasons were understandable, but too often her fellow nurses spent the night out flirting with residents which left them dehydrated and suffering headaches. Hangovers were easily preventable if you abstained from alcohol. Sadie tried a glass of wine once, but hadn't liked the way it made her head spin. Watching others make fools of themselves confirmed she was better off avoiding anything intoxicating.

She pushed the apartment door open to find a familiar face there. Quentin Finnegan.

Sadie tilted her head. "I'm surprised to see you here. What's going on?"

"Craig's in the hospital. He's asking for you." The HSI

supervisor's normally impassive face showed concern. That worried her more than his words.

She wrapped her arms around herself. "What happened? He left me a message last night and said everything was fine."

"He's been shot."

"Shot? By the guy who stole Viper-X? Does that mean he found him?"

"I didn't realize you knew about the biological weapon."

"Madison overheard Matt talking about it."

"Let's take a ride, so you can see Craig."

"I thought he was in Washington."

"He is."

"If I'm leaving town, I need to pack a bag."

"Of course, but make it quick. Our flight leaves in a little over an hour."

"Flight?"

"He took a bullet to the chest, and his condition is critical, I thought you'd want to get there right away, so you can say goodbye if he doesn't make it."

Critical. She hurried up the stairs and into her room. Craig shot. Lying in a hospital bed. Dying. This couldn't be happening. Sadie threw some clothes into a bag while she called work to tell them she wouldn't be in. Then she ran back down the stairs to the waiting SUV.

CHAPTER THIRTY-FIVE

DANTE TAPPED AWAY AT his tabletop screen and Craig rubbed his phone against his thigh.

"What's got you down in the dumps? Shouldn't you be happy that doctor is in custody?"

"I am." Craig sighed. "But Viper-X is out there. They'll use it, and they won't wait long."

"There will always be threats against the country. You didn't cause this, and you're doing all you can to stop the threat, but you can't let it eat at you. Where is that peace that passes understanding?"

"Paraphrasing the Bible now?"

"Only when I think you need to hear it." Dante locked eyes with him. "It's not just the case bothering you. What's under your skin?"

"A woman. I'm going to ask her to marry me but it may mean giving up my career for her."

"Have you prayed about it?"

"Is that your answer to everything?"

"Sure is."

Dante went back to work, and Craig did as he suggested and prayed silently.

Lord, if it be Your will, help me figure out a way to make this thing with Sadie work. She loves me, and I let her down once. Please keep me from hurting her again.

"Hey."

"Find something?"

"I think so. This woman—we only know her as Fiona—has been setting up auctions like this one for years. Her fingerprints are all over this."

"How do we find out who she is?"

"We don't. I pose as a buyer interested in her next auction, and I let her reach out to me."

"What's next on her black-market agenda?"

"She's placing feelers for interested buyers for a stolen diamond."

"Seems rather tame for the same woman responsible for selling a virus that could kill hundreds of thousands if successfully replicated."

"It's a fifteen-carat rare blue diamond. It was taken from the private collection of reclusive billionaire, Edmund Lancaster."

"Do you know how to access the auction?"

"The only way to find out is to get an invitation."

"And you think she's going to invite a CIA officer to her private party?"

"Unlikely, but Gabriel Stanton will show great interest in what she's selling. And will make it known to his contacts that he's interested in the acquisition."

"Who is Gabriel Stanton?"

"Why, I am, of course."

"An alias."

"One of the best."

"You must love your job, dressing up like a billionaire playboy who likes fancy toys. Sounds like a dream job."

"It is. Until the bullets start flying."

"You're going to quite a bit of trouble to help me out."

"That's what friends are for. I know you'd do the same for me. Besides, we've had Fiona on our radar from her weapons deals. She's a big fish for us."

"Maybe our agencies should work together more often. It'd be nice for us both to get a win."

"Sure would." Dante's knee bounced up and down. "I doubt Fiona is in the country though, so we'll have to find a way to draw her here, or I'll have to go to her."

WHEN THEY ARRIVED, SHE ascended the stairs into the airplane. The luxury interior was a nice change from coach, but her stomach was tied up in knots. She couldn't get a signal on her cell phone. Not that she could reach Craig anyway, if he was in surgery. She had to believe he would pull through, or she'd never get through the flight.

Sadie buckled her seatbelt on the private plane. She'd spent the entire drive to Williamsport imagining scenarios where Craig took a bullet and bled out on the ground with nobody there to help him.

"Are you comfortable?" Quentin Finnegan asked as he took the seat across from her.

She nodded. "Thanks for letting me tag along on your flight. It was thoughtful for you to come get me."

"It's what Craig would want."

Sadie wasn't so sure about that. If Craig had his way, she wouldn't know he was ever in danger unless and until he was safe and sound and the threat had passed. He wouldn't want her pacing the waiting room fretting over his well-being, but that was too bad. He didn't get to choose when and where she would love him. It was all or nothing, and she was all in.

Flashes of his demanding kisses the day her mother was rescued replayed themselves. Far better to think on them than the bullet that had torn through his flesh. Why hadn't he been wearing a Kevlar vest? Was it during an operation or had someone come after him when he wasn't expecting gunfire? She had so many questions, but she didn't want to bother Craig's supervisor with them. The last time she'd peppered him with questions back at the wildlife refuge, he'd dismissed her and suggested she get back in the car. Basically, insinuating she should stay out of the way while the grownups did the real work.

Craig was right when he said she had a sensitive heart and soul. The thought of anyone suffering made her weak, but knowing Craig was injured tore her up inside. She should pray, but she couldn't concentrate beyond a plea for help.

CRAIG GLANCED UP FROM his interview with Alhad Sharma as Wally walked into the interrogation room with another FBI agent, Kyle Ash.

"You have something for me?"

"More than you're getting out of him."

"Watching my interrogation techniques so you can brush up on your own?" Craig gave his friend a half smile.

Wally laughed. "You're a little rusty. Let the real men handle your friend here. You have a minute?"

"Sure. He's all yours, Ash." Craig followed Wally into the corridor. "What's new?"

"Dante received his invitation. Auction starts at six. In person."

"Tonight? Where?"

"Yes, tonight. Bahamas."

"That's fast."

"They don't want to leave time between informing the buyers and the sale. Too much time increases the risks for the seller and the broker."

"I'm not sure it's enough time to arrange a bust?"

"For you and me, it wouldn't be, but the CIA has resources we don't."

"Will they be able to get Dante everything he needs to make this happen?"

"Sounds like they've been waiting for an opportunity to insert Gabriel Stanton into a buy like this for some time. He's already in the air on his way to Nassau."

"They do work fast, don't they?" Craig asked.

Wally nodded. "Want to grab lunch?"

"Yes. I don't know when the last time was that I sat down to a meal."

"Old Ebbitt Grill or The Hamilton?"

"Old Ebbitt. And let's walk. I need to get out of this stuffy building."

"The J. Edgar Hoover building is a historical marvel. You should consider yourself privileged to be given the opportunity to interview your suspect inside this hallowed place."

"Have you been drinking the Kool-Aid, Wally?"

"Just a touch. Let me tell Ash we're leaving. He might want to put that monster back in the cage and join us."

Chapter Thirty-Six

Sadie glanced at her phone. It'd been two hours since they took off. Williamsport to DC was only an hour and a half. They may have had to go around some weather, but it seemed like a clear day. She'd watched the weather channel when she was getting dressed that morning and hadn't seen any storms in the area. Strange.

Quentin Finnegan was engrossed in whatever he was reading on his tablet, so he wasn't paying attention to her. She tried tapping out a text message on her phone, but something was blocking the signal from going through. She couldn't access the cell network. Her companion finally glanced up from his work.

"Trouble with the signal? That happens sometimes. We'll be landing soon."

"I was wondering if we'd gone too far to be going to Dulles."

"We're flying into Baltimore." He tugged at his cuff

link. “They took him to Johns Hopkins.”

“Oh.” The knots in her guts tightened. “I thought he was in DC.”

“He’s working out of the DC office, but the accident happened in Maryland.”

Accident. He’d been shot. Didn’t sound like an accident to her. “Accident?”

“Did I say accident, I meant incident. It’s been a long couple of weeks.”

An announcement sounded over the speakers for them to prepare for landing, so she tightened her seatbelt and stuffed her cell in her coat pocket.

Once they landed, they disembarked and the quiet of the fixed-base operator facility struck her. It was so unlike the hustle and bustle of the commercial flight areas. Quentin Finnegan preceded her and the pilot walked behind her. He was intimidating. Probably a bodybuilder with the insane muscles he sported. It was like having her own security detail. A ridiculous thought.

“I need a restroom.” She pointed to a lounge with a sign for a restroom.

“You can hold it until we get to Johns Hopkins,” Craig’s supervisor said.

She danced in place. “I’ve been holding it for hours.”

“Why didn’t you go on the plane?”

“I don’t like using plane restrooms.” She shrugged.

“Fine.” He took her by the elbow and led her through the lounge to a ladies’ room. “I’ll wait for you here. Don’t be long. We need to get going.”

Inside the restroom, she checked her phone’s signal.

It was working. Finally. No new texts from Craig which meant his boss was telling the truth. He would've messaged her by now if he could've. Yet, something didn't feel right. She chewed on her lip a moment. Maybe she should text Craig's coworker, Lisa Harper. The girl was snarky, but she'd know if Craig was shot.

Sadie: Was Craig shot?

Lisa: What?! Not unless it happened in the past hour. He messaged me he was heading to lunch with Wally and would be back in the office this afternoon to prepare for a trip to Nassau.

Sadie: Your boss picked me up. Said we were going to the hospital to see Craig, but he knew I thought we were going to Dulles and didn't correct me until I questioned why we hadn't arrived yet.

Lisa: Where is Finnegan now?

Sadie: Right outside the bathroom door expecting me back.

Lisa: Don't go with him.

Sadie: Why not? He's with Homeland Security.

Lisa: Where are you now?

Sadie: BWI

Lisa: Play along about Craig's injury. Pretend you don't know he wasn't shot. But try to escape. I'll be there as fast as I can. Joel is near you, so he'll get there first. You can trust him.

Sadie: I'm scared.

Lisa: You should be. If he attempts to get you into a car, make as much noise as possible. Scream. Fight. Gouge his eyes out. Whatever it takes.

Sadie: You're not making me feel any safer.

Lisa: Now's not the time for comforting words. Stay alive.

"WHAT'S TAKING SO LONG?" Quentin Finnegan bellowed into the restroom. The only other woman inside turned her way and raised a brow.

The well-dressed woman gave a sympathetic look and clucked her tongue. "That your husband out there?"

"Nope." She took a deep breath and prepared to face the enemy. Why on earth had she believed it was safe to go somewhere with him? He'd rubbed her wrong from the start.

"That was the longest bathroom break in history," Finnegan said.

"I was only in there a few minutes. What's the rush?"

His eyebrows shot up. "Thought you were in a hurry to get to the hospital so you could be by Craig's side?"

"I am."

"Could've fooled me." He grabbed her arm roughly and pushed her ahead of him. Looked like he was switching tactics.

How could she keep him from realizing she knew he'd lied?

"Where is your phone?" he asked.

She patted her pockets. "I must've left it in the restroom. I can go back for it." He gave her a hard shove. "Nice try. Talked to him, huh?"

"Who?"

He shoved her at the pilot. "Clarence, get her to the car. I need to make a phone call." She squirmed as he patted her down and slipped the cell from her inside jacket pocket.

"Time for me to send a message to my former protégé."

CRAIG'S PHONE BUZZED ON the table beside him. He set down his burger and picked it up.

"It's rude to mess around on your phone at the table." Wally pointed at the cell.

"It's a text from Lisa."

Lisa: Sadie's with Finnegan. Needs help.

Craig felt the blood drain from his face. "He has Sadie."

His fingers flew over the keys.

Craig: Where are they?

"He who?"

"Finnegan."

He kept staring at his phone until Lisa's next text came.

Lisa: BWI. On my way there. Joel is five minutes out.

Craig: I'll meet you there.

"What on earth did he abduct Sadie for?"

Craig lifted his eyes to meet Wally's. "Maybe he wants to make a trade. Alhad Sharma for Sadie."

"FBI and HSI will never agree to it. We don't negotiate

with terrorists."

"Right now, he's still my boss."

"Don't even think about it, Craig. You'll not only lose your job. You'll go to prison."

"What would you do if it was your girl?"

"I don't know, but we can't do that."

Another text.

Sadie: I've got your girlfriend. Exchange for my brother at ten. Marina where you met Wally.

"Message from Sadie's number, but it's Finnegan. How does he know I met you at the marina?"

"Maybe he has access to that same AI system Dante uses."

"How?"

"Maybe through a higher-up at Homeland Security. Maybe he also has friends in the CIA. How would I know?" Wally's face scrunched up. "What? You think I'm on his side? You know me better than that."

"You're right. He wants me to doubt you. Divide and conquer, right?"

"Makes sense."

Craig stood. "We can be at BWI in thirty-five minutes."

"With you driving, maybe." Wally tossed some bills on the table, and they rushed from the restaurant, leaving their half-eaten food behind.

They caught a cab back to Craig's car and he tore out of the garage, the brilliant sunshine blinding him. He merged onto I-395 then I-695, weaving in and out of traffic. Wally held the dash and offered a prayer as he drove.

"Lord, let us be in time to help Sadie. Amen."

"You forgot in Jesus' name."

"He knows I mean that part."

"Just say it."

"In Jesus' name, I pray. Amen."

"Thanks. I don't want your prayer hindered from reaching the Father when it could mean the difference between life and death for Sadie."

The car behind him leaned on their horn as he cut them off.

"You're a mental case."

"Sadie said I was a maniac."

"That too."

Chapter Thirty-Seven

Clarence wrapped his meaty hand around her bicep. She pulled away and tried to run. He yanked her back by her hair. "Try that again, and I'll knock out your teeth. I don't care who's watching. Let them make their YouTube videos. Nobody intervenes these days. They just broadcast what they've seen."

"That's not true. There are good people in the world. People who would help." He shoved her through the door and out onto the sidewalk. She screamed. One man stood by filming, but a woman raced toward them. A backhand from Clarence had her flying through the air. Turning on her, he lifted her like a child and carried her to a waiting car. He shoved her into the backseat and climbed in beside her. "Quentin will return soon, and we'll take a ride." He put his hand on her thigh and squeezed. "I think I can come up with a few ways to punish you for your poor behavior."

She spit on him, and he slapped her across the face.

"I don't mind my women a little black and blue. Don't test me, honey."

Quentin opened the door, making a tsk-tsk sound. "Was that necessary, Clarence? Keep your hands off the merchandise."

"I warned her."

"I'm sure you did. I need her in one piece for a fair trade. If Craig decides not to return my brother, you can have her."

Sadie forced herself to breathe evenly and stop fighting. The Lord would provide the opportunity for her to get away, or she would fight back and they'd kill her. But one way or another, she'd escape. By death or by running, she'd get away from these creeps. At least if they killed her, she'd be with Jesus. Tears slipped past her lashes, but she pretended they weren't there, so they wouldn't notice her crying. She could handle her own death, but she knew what it would do to Craig. He'd feel responsible even though it wasn't his fault.

CRAIG PULLED UP TO the curb at the airport and hopped from the car, leaving his emergency light flashing. Wally stayed with him.

He dialed Lisa. "You at BWI yet?"

"Making the turn now. Joel is there. He took video footage from some guy who saw a woman being shoved into a car."

"The guy didn't do anything?"

"Find Joel. I'll be there in two."

He dialed Joel.

"Hey, boss."

"What's up?"

"I'm at the Atlantic Aviation FBO. She was shoved into a car from here. Where are you at?"

"We're at the Signature Flight Support FBO."

"We?"

"I've got Wally with me."

"How fast can you two get over here?"

"Not more than a few minutes."

Craig jumped back into his car and peeled away from the curb.

When they arrived at Atlantic Aviation, they found Joel standing with an Atlantic Aviation employee. "You the guy who took the video?" Wally asked.

The young man bobbed his head up and down.

"Didn't occur to you to help the woman?" Craig asked.

The kid shrugged and Craig had the urge to knock him flat on his rear. "The man who had her looked like a WWF Champion. He'd have snapped me in half."

Craig made eye contact with Joel. "That's not Finnegan."

The kid's eyes grew rounder. "There were two men. The smaller guy looked Middle Eastern, but he didn't have an accent. The big guy had an accent."

"Was it a familiar one?"

"New York, if I had to guess."

"Where is the footage now?"

Joel waved the kid off and handed Craig the phone. "I sent the video to the lab to be analyzed, but he did get a shot of the plate, so I called it in."

"Good."

"What's Finnegan want with Sadie?"

"A trade. For Alhad Sharma."

"He knows we can't do that."

"And he also knows how I feel about her, so he thinks I'll break the rules."

"Oh." Joel rubbed the back of his neck and winced.

"Yeah."

"Boss, I respect you, and I'd do anything for you, so I'm going to help you find your girl, but don't leave me in the dark next time something goes down."

"Lisa told you everything?" He'd asked her to keep it to herself and was kind of surprised to learn she'd breached his trust.

"Someone had to."

"I was keeping things compartmentalized, so I could find out if he had someone inside."

"He did. When Lisa told me last night, I did some digging. And if you'd have brought me in sooner, I could've told you."

"Who?"

"Frederick Collins."

"So, you and Lisa hang out after hours?"

"Don't make more of it than it is. We're friends."

"I didn't know she had any of those." Craig scratched his head. "I feel helpless standing here doing nothing while Sadie's with Finnegan and his hired thug."

Lisa drove up and hopped from her car. "Their vehicle was caught on a red-light camera not ten miles from here."

"He probably ran the red light on purpose to try to bring us to him, so he'd have the advantage," Joel said.

"That is a distinct possibility." Craig rubbed his temples. "He wants to do a trade at the marina."

Wally scratched his chin. "If we can figure out where he is, we can grab her now, but if we don't, we need to make him think you're willing to go ahead with the trade."

"Then he doesn't know Sharma is in FBI custody not Homeland's?" Joel asked.

"I don't know how much he knows. And I can't be sure he doesn't have others on the inside. He somehow knew about my meeting with Wally at the marina."

"When you set up your meeting with Wally, did you call or message from your HSI cell phone?" Lisa asked.

"I did."

"There you have it. He still had his security access when you met Wally. Likely kept tabs on every move you made."

"I never gave details over the phone about what I wanted to meet him about."

"That's likely what tipped Finnegan off. If it was business as usual, you wouldn't have hesitated to say what was going on. Your secrecy let him know you were on to him."

He closed his eyes. "That's why I was so careful to do everything outside of Homeland Security resources."

"But you forgot about the one call you made that set everything else in motion."

Chapter Thirty-Eight

Sadie huddled in the corner of the dank basement where she'd been chained like an animal. Sounds from the upper floors echoed through the plumbing.

Quentin and Clarence talked.

Then Finnegan made numerous telephone calls, setting up his departure plans.

Seemed Finnegan would be long gone before the supposed exchange. His well-paid new buddy, Clarence, was instructed to make the trade and ensure Alhad made it to Tunisia safely.

Once he arrived, Clarence would get the other half of his money. Or so he claimed. The more she got into the brain of criminals the more she understood. And she would put money on the fact that if Clarence ever set foot in Tunisia, he would not be leaving there. It would be his final resting place.

And that morbid thought led her back to her own

predicament. Finnegan was leaving, which meant nobody would be around to rein in Clarence. He'd made his intentions toward her clear, and she'd rather die than endure what he had in mind for her. So, she needed to find a way to escape. There had to be a way to pick the lock keeping the chains on her wrists. Thinking back to the videos she'd watched on lock-picking, she couldn't remember much. And trying her skills at the church hadn't yielded positive results, but she was going to do what she could to get out of this situation. One she wouldn't be in if she'd taken the time to pray and ask God if she should go with Finnegan in the first place.

But that was a useless train of thought. God would be there regardless of her failures. She only needed to lean on Him. She glanced around the floor, hoping for something she could use. An old stool lay on its side. She tugged at her chain, stretching it as far as it would go, so she could reach it, then pulled it closer with her foot. Then she kicked the top from it. Jackpot. A rusty nail stuck out of the legs, giving her something she could use on the lock. Positioning her hands so she could get the nail inserted into the locking mechanism, she worked it inside, but she needed a tension wrench and didn't have one. She pulled a piece of wood from the stool with her teeth and used it to keep the tension while she wiggled the nail inside.

She slipped and bit back a scream as the nail gouged a groove into her cheek. The one still stinging from Clarence's slap.

More talk from upstairs filtered down.

"Once the trade is made and you've secured my brother, grab the little minx again and do whatever you like to her. Just be sure to kill her when you're through, so she can't talk. Not that she knows much, but you can't be too careful." All the more reason for her to get free. No doubt they would follow through.

"Who did you sell the virus to?"

"Not that it's any of your business, but I have no idea. I hit the button to start the auction once I had the case in hand, but all the details were handled by my broker."

"You sold out your country, and you don't even know who to?"

Sadie heard the incredulity in Clarence's voice, and wondered where his ethical line was. He was obviously fine with abusing women, and he didn't mind doing Finnegan's dirty work for a profit, yet he questioned a broker. The man was an enigma.

Forcing herself to keep going, she repositioned the lock and felt for the tiny pins which she had to push up one by one without releasing the tension. It took every ounce of concentration she had. *Lord, help me keep the focus I need and get me out of this place.* She closed her eyes and heard the faint click. She'd done it. The shackle released. Free. Now she needed to find a way out. Light spilled in from a window far above her. If she could get up there, she could shimmy out the window and save herself.

Craig didn't know where she was. He probably thought she was at work. Her only chance of survival was to rely on God to give her the strength to escape.

THERE WAS A WORKBENCH a few feet from the window. Sadie might be able to push it over, but they would hear her. Her best bet was to climb atop it and see if she could reach far enough to grab the edge of the sill and pull herself up. It was a longshot, but it might be her only hope. She reassembled the stool and used it to climb atop the workbench. Extending as far as she could, she still couldn't touch the sill. On her hands and knees, she grabbed for the stool and set it atop the bench. It gave her an extra foot of height, but made leaning to the window even more precarious. Once on top of it, she closed her eyes a second and took a long steadying breath. She stretched out for the window and her fingers brushed it. She grasped for something to hold onto and dug her fingers into the plaster, swinging herself over. Her grip slipped, but she held on with her fingernails and the tips of her fingers and pulled her weight up. It was locked. Fiddling with the lock, she released it. She pushed herself through the narrow space. The window scraped at her midsection as she shimmied through the gap and fell out the other side into a patch of thorny brush. A light flicked on in the basement behind her. They knew she'd escaped and wouldn't be far behind.

Sadie needed to put as much distance between them and her as possible. She ran as if her life depended on her speed. Because it did. A car screeched its tires when she ran out in front of it, but she kept going. Seeing a metal trash can up against a house, she climbed inside and pulled the lid back over herself. The scent of dead fish was strong, but it was better than the alternative. She pinched her nose shut. It gave new meaning to the Bible verse about being still and knowing that He was God. There was little choice inside the can, but to be still and He was her only hope.

She needed them to think she'd kept going. Once they ran past her, she could go for help.

Unsure how much time had passed, she pushed the lid off the can and climbed out, scaring a raccoon as she did. It was too early for it to be out. Rabies was a distinct possibility. She backed away from it and started running in the opposite direction from the way she'd initially come. If they'd seen her leave, they would be looking for her one way, and she would be back the other. After several blocks, she found a woman pushing a stroller. She stopped in front of her and caught her breath.

The grandmotherly woman gave her an odd look. "Strange running attire, dear."

"Do you, by any chance, have a cell phone? I was abducted and need help."

"You ran right past the police station."

"I'd rather call someone I know. My kidnapper has connections."

"I don't have one of those fancy mobile devices, but I do have a landline. Come on inside and you can use it."

Sadie followed the woman and child into the house and made use of the telephone she showed her.

He answered. Thank the Lord. "Craig?"

Chapter Thirty-Nine

"Sadie. Where are you?"

"I don't know. Hold on a second."

"Are you all right?"

"I am. A nice woman let me use her house phone. Can you come get me?"

"Of course, but I need to know where you are?"

"Can you tell him where we are?"

Craig heard murmuring in the background. "She wants to make sure I'm not in trouble with the law. I ran past the police station on my way here."

The woman said, "Hello," on the other end of the line.

"Ma'am, this is Special Agent Craig Malone with Homeland Security. You have concerns?"

"Want to make sure me and my grandbaby aren't in danger by letting this lady stay here," the woman said into the phone.

"Sadie is safe, but the men who may follow her are not.

If you can give me your address, I can come pick her up and minimize the risk to you and your grandchild."

"What if I gave her the keys to my car, and she came to you."

"That'd be fine, but she doesn't have a phone, so if she gets into trouble, she won't be able to call for help." He paused. "Where are you located?"

She rattled off an address not three minutes away from the dock where they were positioned. "We're close. I can be there in a few minutes."

He glanced at his team. "I'm going to pick up Sadie. Stay here and monitor my cell in case he tries to make contact about the exchange. If he doesn't know she's talked to us, he may try to act like he still has her."

"Or she may not have escaped at all. This might be a trick," Lisa said.

"Or he may grab her again if she did escape," Joel said.

"Let's make sure that doesn't happen." Craig gave them a nod and jumped into his car. Wally climbed in beside him. "You're not going without backup."

Two minutes later, he parallel parked at the address he'd been given and slipped from the car. Sadie flew out the front door and down the set of concrete stairs. Craig captured her in his arms, crushing her to his chest.

When he released her, he inspected her for injuries. One side of her face was swollen and cut. "Are you okay?"

"I am now."

Wally patted her shoulder. "Your man has been unbearable since he discovered you were gone."

"My man, huh?" She smiled. "I like that. Was he as bad as I was when my mom was missing?"

"Far worse. It's a miracle his wild ride down I-695 didn't kill us both."

"He's exaggerating." Craig kissed the top of her head, then climbed the stairs so he could thank the woman waiting behind the storm door. She cracked the door open when he reached it. "Thanks so much for letting Sadie wait here." He handed her one of his business cards. "Please call if there is ever anything I can do to help."

"Take care of your wife."

He didn't correct her. "I will." Wife. It was only natural she would assume they were married after the way he'd greeted Sadie, and if he had his way, it wouldn't be long before he made that a reality. A discussion about their future would have to wait until they were alone.

WITH DANTE IN THE Bahamas attending the auction, they didn't have access to Project Sentinel. It was a relief when Lisa suggested Finnegan had simply used HSI technology to listen to his phone calls. It was much less frightening than thinking he had access to the latest CIA technology.

Time was short. If they were going to get Viper-X out of the hands of the buyers and stop it from being used on American soil, they needed to act fast.

A quick glance at his watch told him the auction

should be ending soon, but he needed to arrange a place for Sadie to stay. She could barely hold her head up.

"I think you should have security until we arrest Finnegan. You okay staying at my friend's safe house tonight, or do you want me to get you a hotel room and arrange for security?"

"I can stay at your friend's place."

"I'll be there, too."

"Separate rooms?"

As much as sharing a room might appeal to his baser side, he would wait until they were married. "Of course."

She lifted a shoulder. "Works for me."

His phone rang, and he glanced at the screen. "I have to take this, but as soon as I finish with this call, we'll head back to Dante's place. The team can handle anything more that happens here tonight." It was half past ten and they hadn't received a call from Finnegan, so either he'd given up on the idea of getting his brother released, or he was attempting to work out a new plan. Craig had contacted Brian, so he and Harry were keeping an eye on Craig's parents in case he thought about using them, but Craig didn't think that was likely, and he couldn't think of anyone else Finnegan would try to use to manipulate him.

"Dante, good to hear from you. I'm taking someone else to your safe house tonight, you okay with that?"

"Do whatever you need to do."

"What happened with the auction?"

"You're talking to the winning bidder."

Craig chuckled. "I'll bet that'll tick off the seller when

they learn the CIA bid on their rare blue diamond."

"You know it. We have Fiona in custody. Real name is Tatiana Popova. Russian nationalist."

"She give anything up on the buyers of Viper-X?"

"We're working on it. She gave me a name, but I think he's a go-between."

"Please tell me he's in this country."

"Right there in DC."

"Hmm."

"You thinking what I'm thinking?"

"I'm thinking that means both the buyer and the target are close, too. Which narrows the possibilities for where the attack might take place."

"I'll text you the details so you can get your task force working on it. We'll be getting on a plane within the hour. Grab a couple of hours of sleep, and I'll see you when I see you."

CHAPTER FORTY

CRAIG ASSIGNED TASKS TO everyone and coordinated with the task force to handle finding the go-between and the buyer. He had to catch a few hours of sleep. Wally caught a ride back to his own car with Lisa, leaving Craig alone with Sadie. Finally.

He stole sideways glances as he drove, assuring himself that she was really there and relatively unharmed. He pulled up in front of the log cabin, and she made eye contact.

"There are definitely not two bedrooms in there."

"Trust me."

She gave him a skeptical look, but stepped out of the car when he opened the passenger door. A few minutes later, her eyes widened and her jaw dropped. "This is unreal."

"I had the same reaction when I first saw it."

"Your room is through here. He took her into the

room Wally had used."

"I'll be in the next room if you need me."

"Is it okay if I shower?"

"Absolutely. I'll make us something to eat while you get cleaned up."

She looked down at her scrubs. "I don't have any clothes."

"I'm not going to be a great deal of help there, but I do have some t-shirts and a pair of pajama pants you can sleep in."

"You mean drown in?"

"Something like that." He watched as she disappeared through the door leading to her room before hurrying into the state-of-the-art kitchen and rifling through the cabinets and refrigerator to come up with something to make. A half hour later, he had a spicy beef, black bean, and rice mixture whipped up.

Sadie wandered into the kitchen, looking adorable in his over-sized t-shirt and pajama pants rolled up at the ankles and folded over at the waist. "Dinner smells divine."

"Have a seat." He dished them each up some food and filled two glasses of water.

After he prayed over their food, she dug in, and he did the same.

When she finished eating, she stared blankly at her empty plate before raising her eyes to his. "I am so grateful you weren't shot."

"What do you mean? When would I have been shot?"

"That's how Finnegan got me to go with him. He told

me you were in critical condition. Shot."

"I had no idea." He set his water glass down and took her hands in his. "Lisa told me he had you, but I assumed he'd taken you by force. I didn't know he'd told you that."

"Lisa set me straight when I texted her. Something didn't feel right about the flight, so I wanted to confirm."

He stood and pulled her from her seat and into his arms. "I love you, Sadie. You know that, right?"

She smiled up at him. "I do now."

"Can we talk for a few minutes before you head to bed?"

"Of course."

They settled onto the couch, and she looked up at him expectantly. "I want to make sure we agree about our future before I make plans."

"Our future?"

"If we're going to be together, every decision involves us both from here on out."

"We've only been on three dates, and I'm not sure the second one counts, Craig."

"That doesn't matter. You know me. I know you. If I'm to believe you..."

"And you are."

"Then you've loved me since we were teenagers."

"I have. Though I'm not sure why." She giggled. "You didn't deserve my affection."

"I'm sure I didn't. Still don't, but I'm not willing to let you go again."

"You didn't let me go. You never wanted me."

"Do you remember the night I took you to prom after

that chess geek canceled on you?"

"How could I forget."

"It took every ounce of self-control I possessed to keep from taking what you were offering that night when we were parked by Ridley Lake."

"That was purely physical," she said.

"No, it wasn't. Not for you."

"Okay, you're right. It wasn't." She leaned her head back and closed her eyes. "What's the point in bringing it up now? To complete my mortification?"

"I wanted you, but I wasn't ready to give my heart to someone. As much as I longed to be with you, to love you, I knew I was leaving. A few months later I joined the Navy. I couldn't have been your boyfriend and left you like that. It wouldn't have been fair to either of us."

"When you left, it still hurt."

"I know. And I'm sorry."

"Just don't leave me again."

"That's what I want to talk about."

She pushed away from him on the couch and sat cross-legged. "You're leaving?"

"No. I never want to leave your side again. I don't know how you feel about taking a job in Delaware County, but I was thinking if I took a job working for your father, and you took a job working at a local hospital, we could be together."

She moved closer to him, placing her hand on his knee.

He lifted her hand and kissed her fingers. "Would that work for you?"

"No."

"No?" Craig looked at her like she'd lost her mind. And maybe she had.

"I don't want to have a safe life living in Ridley and never leaving home. You took a job with Homeland Security to make a difference. I'll go wherever your work takes you."

"I wouldn't ask that of you. You deserve stability."

"You're not asking. I'm offering. I won't interfere with your work, so take my offer or don't."

"You'd end things if I said no?"

"Maybe." Her mouth quirked up at the edges.

He kissed the corner of her lips. "You're a liar."

"I'm trying to be noble. Don't ruin it."

"Well, you'd better scurry off to bed now. The temptation of being alone with you is enormous. Almost too much to bear."

"Then I guess you'll have to marry me."

"That's the plan." Her heart did a little skip, and she smiled to herself as she kissed him goodnight. "Now go!"

Back in her room, lying in bed, she let her mind go back to the night after prom. The only night he'd ever kissed her. And, yes, he was correct, she'd been willing to break her chastity vow for him. She'd promised the Lord she'd wait until marriage, but that night with temptation so strong and his arms around her, she would've done whatever he wanted. He'd known about her vow and had stopped things before they'd gone too far. And if she was being honest, she'd have to admit she'd been angry about his decision for a long time.

At the time, it felt more like rejection than kindness, but looking back, she could see the truth. He hadn't wanted to take something precious from her when she'd vowed to wait until marriage. And now, if they married, she would have her purity.

She was under no illusions about his. He'd alluded to a sordid past, and he hadn't been a Christian when he'd joined the military, but she could look past all that and appreciate the goodness in the man even when he'd been a boy. She was glad she'd waited. In no small part, thanks to him.

CRAIG OPENED HIS LAPTOP after Sadie went to bed and researched the name he'd gotten from Dante. What Dante would get in two seconds from Project Sentinel took over an hour of research for Craig. It didn't help that his gaze kept drifting to the bedroom door where Sadie lay sleeping.

Their conversation hadn't gone as expected. He'd thought she would be all in when he suggested moving back to Ridley. He tried to picture her as a Washington DC wife, but the image wouldn't come. She was neither housewife nor politician, but he would support her in whatever she wanted to do whether that was to keep working or to stay home and raise babies. Babies. They could have a brood of their own. Would she want that? He hadn't asked her. He'd always assumed she wanted children, but what if she didn't. Was it a deal breaker for him?

He closed his eyes and pinched the bridge of his nose. Then he strode to the room she was using and knocked on the door. She opened it with a lazy half smile on her face. "Yes?"

"Do you want babies?"

"Now?"

"I'm not asking you to make them right this minute, no, but I want to know if you're open to the idea of having children."

She laughed. "And you thought you should knock on my bedroom door at one in the morning to ask?"

"Did I wake you?"

"What do you think?"

"I think I should let you get some sleep."

"I was awake. After that conversation, I couldn't sleep. I kept replaying prom in my head."

"I'm sorry. I shouldn't have brought it up. We both tried to pretend it never happened. I broke that silent agreement tonight."

She curled her fingers into his t-shirt and tugged him to herself. "I never was able to pretend that night didn't happen." She kissed him gently and took a step back. "And I owe you thanks for keeping me from making a mistake that night."

"You calling me a mistake?"

"No, but giving into what we both wanted would've

been." She pushed the door half closed and spoke through the crack. "Of course, I want kids. Do you know me at all?" The door closed in his face.

Chapter Forty-One

After brushing her teeth with a new brush she found under the sink, Sadie joined Craig in the kitchen. The digital display on the microwave read six o'clock. "Morning."

He drew her into his arms and kissed her. "Good morning, love."

"Any progress on the case?" she asked as she took the coffee he offered.

"Yes, actually. Dante has a lead on a guy that I'm hoping will pan out. He got back here a little while ago and is catching a short nap."

"The life of a CIA officer isn't a quiet one, huh?"

"I suppose it isn't." He lifted his cup to his lips. "Joel is looking into the lead now."

"Does Joel ever sleep?"

"Not often. None of us do when we're neck deep in a case." He rapped his knuckles on the table. "I have some more good news as well."

"What's that?"

"Matt woke up. His mother called this morning."

"Does Madison know?"

"That may be a touchy subject. Matt won't let his mother call her. She keeps calling to check on him, but he doesn't want to talk."

"That's weird."

"Not really."

"What do you mean?"

"I would've felt the same when I was lying helpless in a hospital bed. I wouldn't have wanted you to see me like that. Men don't like looking weak in front of the women they love."

"When were you lying helpless in a hospital bed?"

"Remember I told you about not being able to save my friend who was shot?"

She nodded.

"That's why I couldn't save him. I was bleeding out. Wally and Dante saved me, but they couldn't save him."

"You were shot."

"Multiple gunshot wounds. None fatal."

"Will you show me your wounds?"

He lifted his shirt so she could see a pinkish silver scar on his side. She traced it with her finger. "You can see the others another time."

"I had no idea."

"It's not something I'm proud of."

"But you were wounded serving your country, that's not something you should be ashamed of."

"Not shame, but humility is appropriate, given the circumstances. If I'd been paying closer attention that night when I led my platoon into enemy territory, my friend might still be alive, so it wasn't a shining moment."

"I wish I had been there for you."

"I'm glad you weren't."

She shook her head. "Poor Madison. She must be losing her mind with worry."

"Yeah. Maybe." He smiled. "There is something else I've been meaning to mention, but with all the drama, I kept forgetting."

"What's that?"

"Will you attend an awards ceremony with me next week?"

"What kind of awards ceremony?"

"One where all the bigwigs get together and celebrate themselves while awarding a few honors to the men in the trenches." He sank into his chair and sipped his coffee.

"And are you being awarded?" She walked up behind him and kissed his neck.

"You'd better watch yourself, woman."

"Or what?"

"Or I'll drive you to a chapel now and make you mine tonight."

"I'm already yours. Always have been. But I don't think our parents would appreciate it if we eloped."

"You're probably right." He narrowed his eyes. "So, yay or nay on the banquet next week?"

"I don't have anything to wear to something like that."

"Lisa said she'd help you find something."

"Okay." She lifted a brow. "Lisa doesn't strike me as the shopping type."

"She's not, but she owes me." He laughed. "I already asked her. She'll take you out sometime this week."

"If it wasn't for her warning, I might not have known I needed to try to get away from Finnegan."

"True. But that doesn't let her off the hook for shopping."

"You were confident I'd say yes, weren't you?"

He smiled, but said nothing.

"When is this thing?"

"January 4th. It starts at seven o'clock."

"You never answered my earlier question. Are you receiving an award?"

He shrugged.

"You are, aren't you?"

"It's nothing."

"I'm sure it's something."

FOUR HOURS LATER, DANTE appeared in the kitchen, freshly showered and dressed in a suit and tie.

"I don't know how you can look like you're ready for the cover of GQ four hours after returning home from a mission."

"Someone's got to look this good." Dante grinned. "Got an alert from Project Sentinel. New lead we need to check out."

"What's that?"

"Several men who were supposed to be working various fireworks displays tonight suddenly came down ill with a fast-acting virus."

"Viper-X?"

"We don't know, but if our terrorists want to make something happen at a fireworks show, what better way to accomplish their task than to get their own men on staff. They'll be scrambling for replacements."

"And they'll step in to fill the spots."

"Do we think they'll attack multiple locations at once, or are they planting decoys to thin out our resources?"

"My guess is it's the latter. They would want to disperse it in a single location for maximum effectiveness. Spread it too thin and the effect might not be as severe."

"I'll check with Matt Wright to see what he thinks."

"In the meantime, what do you want to do? I guess we've got to give them what they want. We're going to have to spread our resources thin, so we can cover all the locations where men got sick."

"You and Wally can take the Georgetown Waterfront and I'll take some men and cover the National Mall."

"I'll have Lisa and Joel organize teams to cover the lesser-known events."

"We should have Wally get the FBI's Hazardous Devices Operations Section."

"Calling it by its official name doesn't make you sound smart, Dante. You can refer to them as a bomb squad or use their acronym."

"HDOS. You might be the only person on the face of

the earth that knows what that means."

Craig rolled his eyes. "Let's do this."

Chapter Forty-Two

SADIE PUT HER HANDS on her hips. "I'm going with you."

"It's not safe."

"There is a chance of a deadly virus being transmitted over an enormous crowd, right?"

"Yes! That's why I want you to stay here."

"Who better to have on hand than someone skilled in emergency medical care?"

"This could kill you."

"You're not immune to the threat either."

He rubbed his hands over his face. "For the record, I'm against you having anything to do with this."

"Noted."

He shook his head and climbed into the driver's seat. The woman would be the death of him. Yes, she was a nurse. Yes, she had experience in handling emergency medical situations, but heaven help him, he wanted her safely ensconced in the safe house where nothing could hurt her.

When they arrived on scene, Wally met them at the command post and Craig explained why Sadie had chosen to tag along. "Sadie, I'll take you to the emergency response tent and introduce you to the National Guard team planning to handle the medical response if it becomes necessary. Pray that it doesn't for all of our sakes."

"We should have a prayer tent instead. Much better to ask God to help us stop the threat than to deal with the aftermath if Viper-X is dispersed."

"Amen." Wally clapped him on the back.

Craig frowned as Wally directed Sadie away from him. He hated that he wouldn't be able to concentrate on protecting her, but he had a job to do. Clouds moved in and covered the waning late afternoon sun. If they were correct and the terrorists planned to disperse the virus at midnight, they didn't have much time to stop them.

He went inside the pavilion and cleared his throat. "I need two men checking launchers. I need four men making sure canisters haven't been tampered with." He scanned the crowd, making eye contact with the team one by one. "The rest of you can talk to workers. Find out if anyone has seen anyone suspicious. I want to know the second you hear anything you think might be relevant."

THE CHURNING IN SADIE's stomach grew worse with each passing hour as she waited with the rest of the medical staff for something to go wrong. A phone call from Madison had her stepping outside the tent, grateful for something to do other than wait.

"Hey, Maddie."

"Did you know Matt was awake?" No preamble or niceties.

"Not until this morning."

"And you didn't call me?"

"I've been kind of busy."

"Too busy to care what I'm going through?"

"That wasn't how I meant it."

"I drove down to the hospital to see him, and he's been released. Released! And they won't tell me where he is."

"He's here."

"What do you mean he's there?"

"They're expecting a terrorist attack tonight with the biological weapon that was stolen from the New Mexico lab. The one Matt developed the antidote for."

"I guess it's a good thing the government has the antidote then, huh?"

"What do you mean? They don't have it."

"Yes, they do. Matt gave it to me to hide. I gave it to Homeland Security the day of the attack at the John Heinz wildlife refuge."

"Who, precisely, did you give it to?"

"Craig's boss. Some kind of big-shot supervisor."

"Quentin Finnegan?"

"Yeah. Him."

Sadie shook her head. "I need to let Craig know that. Not sure we can do anything about it now, but Finnegan is dirty."

"Would you tell Matt to call me?"

"Yes. I will." Provided they all lived through the night. Sadie rested her head against the tent post and sucked in a few breaths. A scuffle nearby drew her attention. A tall man shoved a shorter frail guy.

"Where are the canisters?"

"In the trunk. I couldn't bring them in past all this security."

"You're useless. You know that?"

The man pointed to a roasted chestnut cart sitting by itself with nobody around. "Grab that cart over there. You can bring them in on that."

"I'm allergic to chestnuts."

"Do I look like I care?"

Sadie waited, her heart beating frantically. When their steps faded away, she called Craig. Right to voicemail. She waited a few minutes and tried again. Same result.

She ran, the cold air burning her lungs. She had to make it to the command pavilion before midnight. Struggling for air, she bent at the waist and tried to get control of her breathing. Craig was nowhere to be seen, but she spotted Wally with several other men. Tugging on his arm until she had his attention, she forced her words to come out slowly so they weren't tripping over themselves. "They're going to bring the canisters in on a cart that sells roasted chestnuts."

"How do you know that?" Wally asked.

"Overheard two guys."

"We're on it. Good job, Sadie."

He picked up a radio and relayed the information to the team.

CRAIG LOOKED AROUND. No chestnut carts.

Kevin ran toward him and pointed. "I think I found the cart."

"Why didn't you use your radio?"

"They would've heard me."

"Let's go." Craig spotted the cart a few feet from the shed where they were filling the loaders with canisters. He locked eyes with Kevin. "Go back to the pavilion and tell Wally we need the bomb squad at the fireworks shed." Not wanting to incite a panic, he strode toward the shed, his movements quick and purposeful, but not frantic. When he reached the shed, he bent close to the fire chief. "Bomb squad is on site. They'll be inspecting the canisters one by one before they can be shot."

"We've been expecting them."

"The latest intelligence suggests the attack will originate from here."

A man loaded canisters into launchers a few feet from where the two of them stood. Craig watched. Something didn't seem right. He turned back to the man, and the guy took off at a run. "Wally, our man is on the move."

Sadie appeared in the doorway.

"What are you doing here?"

"Finnegan. He's here."

"Where?"

"Hanging by the medical tent."

Quentin Finnegan appeared over Sadie's shoulder. "Not any more, I'm not. Your sweet little pet escaped me last time, Craig, but I have her now. If you want her to live, you'll get my brother."

"I'll shoot you before you can do a thing to her."

"Yes, you might, but these canisters in here, they're the decoys. The real ones are going off at the National Mall. I saved enough of the virus to share it with a select few, and I've already infected Sadie."

"You're bluffing."

"Am I?" Finnegan chuckled. "I have the antidote. Got it from Dr. Wright's girlfriend."

Sadie's countenance fell. Did she know something he didn't?

Chapter Forty-Three

Sadie watched as Finnegan sauntered through the crowd. Nobody attempted to stop him. "Why are you letting him get away? I'm not sick. He didn't infect me with anything."

"How can you possibly know that? All he had to do was spray some into the air near where you were."

A call came through on his radio, and they both listened. Several people had collapsed at the medical tent.

"We need to get that antidote from him."

Wally sauntered up. "Bomb squad checked the canisters. Duds."

Craig called Dante. "Looks like you're up. Finnegan showed up. Claims the real threat is at the National Mall."

"We need to stop Finnegan and find out if he has the antidote on him before we lose anyone to this virus," Wally said.

Sadie snapped her fingers. “Where is Matt?”

“Last I saw him, he was at the command post.”

“He gave the vials to Madison. She gave them to Finnegan, but what if he kept some. If it were me, I wouldn’t have given away all my research. And if I knew I was coming to the place where there might be an attack, I’d have it on me.”

“That sounds like a longshot.”

“Worth asking him.”

A wave of dizziness hit her. “I need to sit.”

“Wally, he wasn’t bluffing. Get Dr. Wright over to the medical tent now.”

He covered Sadie’s face with an N95 mask he’d had stuffed in his pocket, then lifted her into his arms and carried her back to the medical tent where he laid her on a cot. Matt pulled his wheelchair up beside her.

CRAIG MADE EYE CONTACT with his friend. “How long does she have, Matt?”

“There is no set time, but I’d guess less than twenty-four hours.”

“Do you have any of the antidote on you?”

“I don’t, but when I gave it to Madison, I gave her two extra vials of antidote and told her to get them into a safe place.”

“Call her. We need it.”

“I’ll sit with Sadie, while you go to the National Mall.”

“Wally told you.”

"He did," Matt said.

Craig took one last look at Sadie. He bent to kiss her, but Matt put his hand between them. "You could infect everyone. You're already going to be a risk. Go take care of the threat. If you want to infect yourself, wait until after you've saved those you can."

Craig didn't like hearing it, but Matt was right. He had a duty to his country. As he drove to the National Mall, he begged the Lord for the strength to get through the night.

Dante directed him where to go through radio communication, and the two met up at the staging area for the fireworks. "We've got five minutes to stop this."

"We didn't stop it. Sadie's infected."

"Wait, what?"

"Like you said, we have five minutes. Show me what you need me to do."

"Those launchers have been checked." Dante swept his arm toward a group of men set up with fireworks launchers.

The first firework was released. It exploded into the air, and red-and-gold lights rained down on the mall. It was magnificent, but it meant time was up. Craig caught something out of the corner of his eye. "That guy there is switching out his canister." Craig pointed. "Is that expected?"

"No, it's not." Dante started running toward him.

Craig followed as Dante tackled the guy, bringing him to the ground. The man pulled a handgun and took a wild shot, catching Dante in the side, and scrambling away.

Craig bent over his friend.

"I'll live. Chase him."

Craig took off and dove on top of the suspect, using a leg sweep to knock his feet out from under him. He went down hard.

"You'll never stop us," the man said as Craig cuffed him. "We'll keep coming at you until we win."

"It might be like patching a leaking dam with a bit of pitch, but we won't give up trying to put monsters like you in prison where you belong."

He wrenched the guy up to his feet and shoved him into the arms of a waiting FBI agent. "HSI is keeping this guy, but you can put him in holding."

Craig went back to where he'd left Dante. Medics were patching him up. "You all right?"

"I will be. Get back to Sadie."

Craig gave a slight nod. "I will, but I'll be by to see you later." They loaded Dante into the back of the ambulance, and Craig watched the bomb squad loading up canisters.

The crowd would be disappointed that the fireworks display was cut short, and they'd never know why, but they'd averted one of the biggest threats to ever hit American soil. Made in America by an American.

CRAIG SAT BESIDE SADIE in the hospital and held her hand. Her eyelids flickered open. "Where am I?"

"Johns Hopkins."

"That's ironic. I was supposed to visit you there when I thought you'd been shot. What happened?"

"You don't remember?"

She shook her head.

"Finnegan infected you with the virus. It was touch and go for a while there, but Madison drove straight here when you told her that Finnegan was dirty and that Homeland didn't have the antidote. Apparently, Matt had given her a couple of extra vials to put aside."

"What about the others who were infected?"

"Nobody is going to die from the virus."

"The attack in the fireworks?"

"Averted."

"I'm so glad."

"Me too. Rest." He bent down and kissed her eyelids.

Chapter Forty-Four

Craig couldn't tear his eyes away from Sadie as they ate their salads. The blue gown she wore was lined with sequins and hugged her curves without being revealing. Matt Wright sat beside him in a wheelchair.

After the meal, the Director of Homeland Security Investigations introduced the Secretary of Homeland Security. Craig sat up straighter. He hadn't realized the secretary would be present for this.

The man talked about the fabulous work of the men and women under his purview, then cleared his throat. "It is my honor to present the Distinguished Service Medal to Special Agent Craig Malone for his extraordinary service and bravery in the face of an unparalleled threat against our country. His actions led to the capture of traitors and the safe retrieval of a deadly weapon."

Not surprisingly, the secretary did not mention any specifics about the biological nature of the weapon or how close it had come to being dispersed along with the fireworks over the Georgetown Waterfront when the clock struck midnight to ring in the New Year. Craig rose and strode up to the stage to receive the award. The secretary shook his hand, and he looked out over the crowded room. "Couldn't have accomplished this without my team and the exceptional task force." He hurried back to his seat.

Sadie smiled and took his hand.

He needed to get her down to the altar sooner rather than later. Last night he'd driven to Ridley to ask her father for her hand. The older man welcomed him to the family with tears in his eyes, claiming he'd always hoped Craig and Sadie would find their way to each other.

Now Craig sat beside the love of his life, diamond in the pocket of his tux, waiting for the right moment to ask her to be his wife. They'd talked about a future, but tonight he would make that commitment with a ring.

"What's on your mind?" She rested her hand on his arm.

"You."

Her cheeks flushed an adorable shade of pink. "You're lying. What were you thinking about just now?"

He pulled out the diamond and knelt down on one knee in front of her. "Will you marry me, Sadie Kline?"

"Yes!" She held out her hand as he slipped the ring on.

He stood and dragged her close, kissing her, and the tables nearby all clapped. It'd been his plan to wait until they had a private moment after the banquet, but her questioning his thoughts made him impatient to ask.

"How long will it take you to plan a wedding?"

"Depends on how elaborate we want it to be."

"Would you mind keeping it simple?"

"Not at all."

"Three months work for you?"

"Six."

"Okay, fine. Six months, but not a day more." He kissed her again.

LISA SAT BETWEEN SADIE and Joel at the awards ceremony, but her gaze kept flitting to Dante. What was he even doing there? It wasn't like he worked for HSI or even ICE. He wouldn't talk about which of the three letter agencies he worked for, but she knew. She didn't need anyone to tell her that he was CIA. Everything about the man screamed covert operator.

She couldn't understand how anyone who claimed to have religion could take a job where they lied for a living.

It wasn't her style, and she didn't subscribe to a higher power. She had to admit though, Craig had a peace about him she longed for. If he got that from his God, maybe his God was worth knowing. Wally and Dante both seemed to have that inner calm, too.

Dante locked eyes with her before leaning down to whisper in her ear. "Like what you see?"

She punched his shoulder. "I'm wondering what you're even doing here."

"Shot in the line of duty on a joint operation." He

grinned. "I get bonus kudos for that."

"It was barely a scratch."

"An award-worthy scratch." Dante rubbed his chin, his eyes alight with mischief.

She patted his hand in a patronizing way, but the spark that sizzled between the two of them had her pulling back. Dante was the kind of guy her mother warned her about. Too good-looking for his own good. Probably had a woman in every town where he had an alias. And she was guessing he had plenty of those.

Also By Elle E. Kay

Project Sentinel (coming soon)

Toxic Truths
Midnight Offensive
Midnight Masquerade (coming soon)

Pennsylvania Parks Series
Grave Pursuits
Grave Secrets
Grave Consequences

Endless Mountain Series
Shadowing Stella
Implicating Claudia
Chasing Sofie

Heroes of Freedom Ridge Series

Healing the Hero
A CHRISTIAN ARMY RANGER CHRISTMAS ROMANCE
Persuaded by the Hero
A CHRISTIAN ARMY VETERAN CHRISTMAS ROMANCE
Inspired by the Hero
A CHRISTIAN PHYSICIAN ASSISTANT CHRISTMAS ROMANCE

Christmas in Redemption Ridge Series
Wooing the Widower
Corralling the Cowboy

Blushing Brides Series
The Billionaire's Reluctant Bride
The Bodyguard's Fake Bride

The Lawkeepers Contemporary Romance Series
Lawfully Held
A K-9 LAWKEEPER ROMANCE
Lawfully Defended
A SWAT LAWKEEPER ROMANCE
Lawfully Guarded
A BILLIONAIRE BODYGUARD LAWKEEPER ROMANCE

The Lawkeepers Historical Romance Series
Lawfully Taken
A BOUNTY HUNTER LAWKEEPER ROMANCE
Lawfully Given
A CHRISTMAS LAWKEEPER ROMANCE
Lawfully Promised
A TEXAS RANGER LAWKEEPER ROMANCE

MIDNIGHT OFFENSIVE

Lawfully Vindicated
A US MARSHAL LAWKEEPER ROMANCE

Standalone Novella
Holly's Noel

Reader Letter

Dear Reader,

Thank you for picking up *Midnight Offensive.* I hope Craig and Sadie's story kept you turning pages long past bedtime!

Enjoyed it? I'd be grateful if you'd share a few honest sentences on your favorite online store or wherever you like to post reviews—every bit of feedback helps other suspense-loving readers discover the book.

Hunting for your next read? You'll find my complete catalog—and a sneak peek at upcoming releases—on the "Novels" page at ElleEKay.com. **Join my reader family** to receive a free ebook, behind-the-scenes farm updates, and early sale alerts. You can sign up right from my website's homepage.

Happy reading, and God bless!

Elle E. Kay

About Author

Angel Award–winning novelist Elle E. Kay spins the stories she loves to read: edge-of-your-seat suspense threaded with heartfelt faith and swoon-worthy romance. She and her husband run a hobby farm in Pennsylvania's Appalachians, where three exuberant dogs keep watch over goats, chickens, and the rest of the barnyard crew. When she isn't embroiling her characters in danger, Elle sings in her church's music ministry, teaches a teen Bible class, and soaks in the beauty of nearby Red Rock Mountain.

Since her 2016 debut, Elle has penned more than two dozen books—including the reader-favorite *Pennsylvania Parks* and *Endless Mountain* series—and contributed to popular multi-author projects such as *The Lawkeepers*, *Blushing Brides*, *Heroes of Freedom Ridge*, and *Christmas in Redemption Ridge*.

Her latest release, *Midnight Offensive* (Book 1 in the

Toxic Truths series), launches a pulse-pounding thriller arc packed with high stakes, unexpected twists, and the enduring hope of the gospel.

Under the pen name Ellie Mae Kay, she also writes farm-themed picture books that capture the charm of rural life for young readers.

You can connect with Elle on her website at https://www.elleekay.com/ or on social media:

Facebook: www.facebook.com/ElleEKay7

Instagram: www.instagram.com/elleekay7

Personal Testimony

I first came to know Jesus as a young teen, but before long I strayed from God and allowed my selfish desires to rule me. I sought acceptance and love from my peers, not knowing that only God could fill my emptiness. My teen years were full of angst and misery for me and for my family. People I loved were hurt by my selfishness, and the heartache was at times overwhelming. After several runaway attempts, my family was left with little choice, and they placed me in a group home / residential facility where I would receive the constant supervision I needed.

At that home, I met a godly man called "Big John," who tried once again to draw me back to Jesus. He pointed me to Matthew 11:28-30 and reminded me that all I had to do to find peace was give my cares to Christ. I wanted to live a Christian life, but something kept pulling me away. The cycle continued well into adulthood: I would call out to God, and then I would turn away from Him. (If you read the Old Testament, you'll see that the nation of Israel had a similar pattern: they would call out to God and He would heal them and bring them back into their land. Then they would stray, and He would chastise them. It was a cycle that went on and on.)

When I finally realized that God's love was still available to me despite all my failings, I found a peace and joy that have remained with me to this day. It wasn't God who kept walking away. He had placed His seal on me in childhood, and no matter how far I ran from Him, He remained faithful. When I recognized His unfailing love, **I was made free.**

> 2 Timothy 2:13
> "If we believe not, yet he abideth faithful: he cannot deny himself."

> Ephesians 4:30
> "And grieve not the holy Spirit of God, whereby ye are sealed unto the day of redemption."

I let myself be drawn into His loving arms and led by His precious nail-scarred hands. He has kept me securely at His side and taught me important life lessons. Jesus gave me back the freedom I had in Christ on that day when I accepted the precious gift He offered. My life in Him is so much fuller than it ever was when I tried to live by the world's standards.

I implore you: if you've known Jesus and strayed, call out to Him.

If you've never known Jesus Christ as your personal Lord and **Saviour**, find out what it means to have a relationship with Christ—not religion, but a personal relationship with a loving God.

God makes it clear in His Word that there isn't a person righteous enough to get to heaven on their own.

> Romans 3:10
> "As it is written, There is none righteous, no, not one:"

We are all sinners.

> Romans 3:23
> "For all have sinned, and come short of the glory of God;"

Death is the penalty for sin.

> Romans 6:23
> "For the wages of sin is death; but the gift of God is eternal life through Jesus Christ our Lord."

Christ died on the cross for our sins.

Romans 5:8
"But God commendeth his love toward us, in that, while we were yet sinners, Christ died for us."

If we confess and believe we will be saved.

Romans 10:9
"That if thou shalt confess with thy mouth the Lord Jesus, and shalt believe in thine heart that God hath raised him from the dead, thou shalt be saved."

Once we believe He sets us free.

Romans 8:1
"There is therefore now no condemnation to them which are in Christ Jesus, who walk not after the flesh, but after the Spirit."

I hope you'll take hold of that freedom and start a personal relationship with Christ Jesus today.

All Scripture quotations are taken from the Authorized Version of the Bible, commonly known as the King James Version (KJV).